The Lost Farm

The
Lost Farm

Jane Louise Curry

Illustrated by Charles Robinson

A Margaret K. McElderry Book

ATHENEUM 1974 NEW YORK

J cop. 2

For Marnie, with love—
and for Quentin, who was
too young to go along.

One

IN MAY OF 1922 PETE MACCUBBIN WAS TWELVE YEARS old, the best hitter on the sixth-grade baseball team, an expert jackknife flipper, an avid reader of the works of Mr. Mark Twain and Mr. Ring Lardner, and the most miserable human being in Summit County, Pennsylvania, U.S.A., The World, The Universe.

"Twelve year old, eh?" his father, Trashbin Mac-Cubbin had drawled in between swallows of the apple spice cake Granny made only on special occasions. "Wal, then, 'bout time you give up this school nonsense, ain't it? I been wanting a full-time hand on the place so's I can get out and around more'n I do. Expand the business." He ignored Granny's snort. "You tell that principal-lady you won't be back come autumn. Tell her your Paw needs you. Now, you got no call to go pulling a long face at me, Petey boy. I know what I'm about. I been all the way to the eighth grade, and it never done me one lick of good."

" 'Cause you never had one lick of sense," Granny snapped. But not even Granny could budge Donalbain MacCubbin when he dug his heels in. In Mosstown and up and down the country he was called "Trashbin," both because he had taken up old Horsefeathers Mac-Cubbin's trade (if you could call it that) of collecting "vallable trash," and because he generally looked as if he had slept in a trash barrel. His own daddy, Horse-feathers' son Malcolm, had won Granny's hand in marriage with his light heart and good looks, brought her from Chambersburg to the homestead on White Oak Ridge, and then got himself killed at Gettysburg before his baby boy had learned to say "Papa." Instead, the boy Donalbain learned at old Horsefeathers' knee to say "Gol darn!" and "I'm a ringtail roarer" and other pithy expressions painful to Granny's ears.

Old Horsefeathers was a hero to the little fellow, and Granny might as well have packed up and left for California on her lonesome for all the heed they paid her, but she was as stubborn as the both of them and never did give up trying. Trashbin, grown-up, had a kind of lazy-mean streak that would have dismayed the old man, but the old man died at the respectable age of one hundred three, leaving his grandson the wagon and mules and an impressive collection of jugs and old iron. Being of sound mind, the old man had left the farm and the livestock to his daughter-in-law.

With the farm safe, Granny had been able to breathe easy at last, even as she sighed over Trashbin's grow-ing bottle collection and the stacks of magazines and old iron that threatened to crowd the cattle out of the barn. Trashbin was convinced that "Pretty soon these here writers'll be wrote out, and when there ain't nothing new to be said and they stop printing books and such, why, folks as haven't read 'em'll pay good money for these old magazines. You mark my words: five or ten year from now, that'll be a Vallable Collection." And while he rummaged in Mosstown's trash barrels, it was Granny who hitched up the mule team, plowed the north field, south field, and kitchen garden, harrowed them, and planted clover for hay, mangels for winter feed for the stock, and both field corn and sweet corn, and grew a whole alphabet of vegetables and flowers from asparagus to zinnias.

The moonlit September night when Trashbin appeared with a girl perched at the back of the wagon atop a stack of *Saturday Evening Posts*, and announced that they were married, began one of Granny's happiest times. Maybelle was a little peaky thing, nervous and pale, and needing all the love and feeding Granny pressed upon her. It turned out Trashbin had found her rummaging for food in the trash barrel behind Banks' Hotel in Mosstown, for she'd run away from the County Orphanage, where she'd been kept on as a kitchen slavey from the time she turned seventeen. Granny would have liked to think Trashbin had a touch of real fondness for the girl, but she suspected it was finding her rummaging in a trash barrel that had set his mind on her. Anyway, the following June Petey was born, and Maybelle died, as quiet and easy as if she was a bit of dandelion fluff the breeze had blown away. All Granny's coddling and cream cheese and nourishing soups hadn't been much help. Trashbin proved himself even meaner than the dreaded cook in the County Orphanage kitchen, so when Maybelle saw how sick she was, she took her chance and died of it.

Young Pete, the apple of his granny's eye, showed good sense from the first and hid under the front steps when his daddy drove scowling and growling up the road before suppertime and under Granny's bed if he came rolling and roaring in late at night.

Trashbin, hardly ever seeing the boy, three-quarters of the time forgot he was there. When he did recall it, he rolled up his sleeves and gave the boy a good switching, "To Learn the Boy to Respect his Daddy." Or else he took away the long-saved-for mouth organ or the treasured bag of aggies and blue glass marbles, "To Learn the Boy it was a Hard World." Now he was taking away school, "To Learn the Boy he Didn't Need No Learning."

Young Pete dragged his bare feet through the dust because he liked the warm silky feel of it. The first three miles of the way home from school were hard because there was only the hot tar of the asphalt or the sharp-edged gravel along the shoulder of the road to walk on, and it was worth your hide to put your good boots on and go shod. Boots were for church and school, and you took them off directly you got past the lilacs at the corner of the schoolyard. That way they were still practically new when you grew out of them, and Granny could get a better trade-in when she took you to the shoemaker for new ones. After the turnoff onto the dirt road below Inkle's Springs, though, the boots slung over your shoulder and tied together by their laces were no longer a temptation. You walked in one of the deep ruts—it was a little like walking along a fence rail, the way you had to balance—and let the dust sift between your toes.

At Inkle's Springs, shade trees lined both sides of the road, and in the unmown grass, blue and yellow irises crowded along the fence where the climber roses were already heavy with buds. Past the old Sampson barn, the road came out from under the trees and tilted up across the fields that hadn't been plowed and planted since Old Man Sampson passed on the year before. His son, a druggist up in Hoxey, had fancied himself too refined to get calluses on his hands from working the land, so the old place stood empty, with a "For Sale" sign nailed on the front gatepost.

Because there was no one to mind, young Pete took a drink from the tin cup at the spring in the overgrown Sampson garden and soaked his feet a while in the little stream. Then, because he had no need to hurry and because the road up across the fields swam in the sultry heat, he found a soft tuft of grass in the shade of the birch tree by the barn door, and settled down, propped against the barn wall, to read a bit of *A Tour of the Moon* by Mr. Verne. Miss Ample, who was both sixth-grade teacher and principal at Mosstown School, had been upset at the news that Pete would not be going on to seventh grade and had promised to lend him books whenever he could get into town. He had picked Mr. Verne because of the fantastic title, and because the book was not too fat to hide under his shirt. Trashbin didn't like him reading at home. Now, settled down comfortably with the volume propped on his knees, he was soon deep in the adventures of the three members of the Baltimore Gun Club who were fired in a great projectile to the moon.

"*Must* you turn the pages so fast?" complained a small voice in his ear.

Pete jumped up, slamming the book shut, and looked up and down the road.

There wasn't a soul in sight, Paw or anyone else. Not that the high piping voice had been the least like Trashbin's gravelly roar, but Paw always did love to make him jump like a scared rabbit. Pete pulled up his shirt and stuffed the book under his belt, taking no chances. Trashbin had had his eye on the window glass and hardware at the Sampson place, and already a dozen or so panes, a boot-scraper, and the front and back doorknobs were missing from the house. In the barn there was a goodish plow and harrow and a lot of harness. Maybe his old man was fixing to steal that. Now that Pete looked, he saw fresh wagon tracks in the dust of the turnoff to the barn, and with a sinking feeling he guessed that the MacCubbin wagon was inside, with Trashbin loading up "a few of them things nobody wants."

He was wrong. Not only was there a shiny new Yale padlock on the big barn doors, but a quick trip around the barn revealed new padlocks on both side doors and brown paper pasted over the ground-floor windows. "Golly, who in thunder'd want to do that?" he marveled. It wasn't like Mr. Sampson, Junior, who never paid the place any mind, and the sheriff, when he sealed up a place the county meant to auction off for the back taxes, always nailed up a special notice. Pete walked back around to the big, sliding doors and put his eye to the crack between them. From inside came the soft, unmistakable nicker of a horse.

There were two horses—big bays—in the stalls where Old Man Sampson had stabled his mules; and in the center of the open threshing floor stood a huge gaily colored circus wagon. Circus or gypsy, whatever it was, it bore an elegant freshly painted sign along its side: *Professor Lilliput and His Marvelous Museum of Miniatures.*

"Gee whillikers!" Pete drew in his breath. What could it mean? Mosstown was scarcely big enough to draw a carnival for two days in August, so the wagon couldn't belong to a circus, and the gypsies always camped at Schaffer's meadow when they came through, and they had dozens of babies and barking dogs. What it looked most like was an old-time traveling show straight out of an old-fashioned picture book—the kind that had a fake Indian and a magician who sold tonic and rheumatism cures on the side.

Pete cocked an eye up at the high window-door into the haymow, sagging on its hinges, and grinned. After all, there was no "Keep Out" sign, and Old Man Sampson, when he was alive, had never minded him playing in the barn. "Just a peek," he told himself, as he skinned up the birch tree.

Once level with the haymow door, Pete pried it open with one foot, and swung himself in. The hayloft ran around three sides of the barn, above the stalls and storage area. The middle was open from the ground to the rafters, so that by moving to the east end of the loft Pete could look down and into the open doors at the rear of the wagon.

On each side, wide shelves ran from front to back, one about a yard above the wagon floor, the next two and a half feet above it. Along these shelves, and along the floor beneath them, were lined up miniature shops and houses, a small barn, and a stable-garage or two, for all the world like shops and houses along a real street. There was a bank, an inn, a general store, even a church. Directly below the edge of the loft, as Pete could see when he stretched out flat on the dusty floor and peered over, planks had been set across two wooden sawhorses to make a trestle table. On it stood a handsome little stone house, near a glue pot and a heap of small stones apparently intended for patching its second, broken chimney. At the other end of the table, atop a litter of brushes and jars of paint, several placards had been set to dry.

One card read *Please Do Not Touch the Exhibits. They have been Collected at Great Expense and Newly Refurbished for your Enjoyment. Several I have, taking Great Pains, made Myself, Endeavoring always to Please and Astound.* It was signed with an elaborate flourish, *Professor Lilliput, M.A., Ph.D.* Another was more direct: *Admission: Kiddies—5¢, Ladies and Gentlemen over 12 yrs. of Age—25¢.* The third announced that Professor Lilliput would arrive in the Fair Metropolis of Mosstown at ten on the morning of the first Saturday in June for a Grand Send-off of the Museum's second Transcontinental Tour.

A week from tomorrow. But twenty-five cents! Being twelve years old was expensive. There was, of course, the dollar twenty-five he had saved toward a dollar seventy-five Keen Kutter pocketknife, but if he spent a quarter now, at the rate Granny doled out nickels, he'd be an old man before he got the knife. It wouldn't take but a minute to slip down the ladder for a close look now. . . .

But if he got caught, he'd be turned over to Constable Dudley, and Paw would whale the tar out of him for "Bringing Disgrace on the Family" (which would be unfair, seeing how often Trashbin had been locked up in the town jail, usually by Constable Dudley). Pete considered. There *was* a three-bladed Boy Scout knife at Dean's Emporium for a dollar. It wasn't as good as a Keen Kutter, but having it sooner would make up for that. Relieved—for sneaking always made him feel small and about-to-be-stepped-on—he went out and down the way he had come, wedging the door shut behind him.

There was still no one in sight down the road, so Pete pulled his book out from under his belt, plumped back down on his grassy seat, and prepared to settle back into *A Tour of the Moon*. If anything was better than Mr. Twain or Mr. Lardner, whose stories made you laugh, it was stories of strange places and impossible adventures.

"It's a *very* interesting story, but you'd really better go," piped a trill of a voice in his ear. "The Professor and his horrid nephew will be coming back any time now."

Petey rose, whirling to face the barn wall behind him. There, leaning out through a knothole just above where his shoulder had rested, was a skinny little girl in pigtails, all of five inches tall.

"I'm Samantha," she said, quite conversationally. "And you can come back tomorrow after lunch. They'll be gone again then. *Please* go."

When it became apparent that Petey was too amazed and fascinated to do any such thing, she gave a sigh. "Well, if I'm going to have to 'make a long story short,' you'd better sit down again, or I'll get a crick in my neck."

Two

HE HAD IMAGINED IT, OF COURSE. HE TOLD HIMSELF SO for the twelfth time: he had dozed over the book and dreamed it all. It wouldn't hurt to go back tomorrow after lunch, though, just to make sure. It had been so real—and so different from his everyday daydreams about becoming a daredevil aviator or winning a Daisy air rifle in the Volunteer Fire Company's Fourth of July picnic raffle.

"Granny?" he whispered cautiously, keeping an ear tuned to the *creak-creak* of Trashbin's rocker on the front porch. "There ain't truly such a thing as fairies, is there?"

"Land sakes, what a question! Of course not." Granny fished another dish out of the rinse pan for him to dry. "Fairy tales are like meringue-cake—right pretty and sweet to the tooth, but mostly just air."

The tiny little girl had not been at all pretty or sweet or airy. She was, in fact, snippy like any ordinary girl, and everything she said had seemed perfectly sensible at the time. But now . . . . He wriggled his shoulders uncomfortably and said, "Shoot, Granny, I know there isn't really such a thing. But, say if there *was*—how big would they be?"

Granny considered as she scoured the iron frypan. "Now that's hard to tell. Some stories make them out no bigger'n my thumb, but in the old Scottish ballads my auntie sang when I was a girl, they were always as tall as humans. Only *different*. Seems the little wee fairies are mostly in the made-up stories, not in the tales that have growed up out of superstition and been passed down from long ago."

Petey was relieved. Samantha had insisted that she was as ordinary a human being as he was, but he had been uneasy just the same. Now only the possibility that he *had* dreamed it all kept him from pouring out the story to Granny. Granny had the warmest of hearts, but she had little patience with softheadedness. Then, too, the creaking on the front porch had stopped.

Professor Lilliput's real name (as the tiny Samantha had explained after Pete had ignored her urgings to flee) was Willie Kurtz. And Willie Kurtz had accidentally invented a Reducer, a dreadful machine that shrank whatever it was aimed at. He had made medical machines before—the Patented Gallstone Dissolver, a Circulation Stimulator, and a Vital Ray Diagnostician —but though they hummed and flashed impressively and earned him a tidy living from his "patients," and though he genuinely believed in them himself, they really did nothing but hum and flash. The Wart and

(15)

Malignant Growth Reducer, to give it its full name, was different: two wires accidentally crossed, then a condenser innocently attached, a generator coil that was actually connected—and the Reducer, astonishingly, reduced. First it reduced a wall in the Professor's workroom to baseboard height, which was rather inconvenient; then a tree across the road, as well as the flowerpot he had aimed for on the workroom windowsill. Unfortunately, the focus control could not be adjusted for anything smaller than a bakery truck and so, as far as shrinking warts went, it was quite useless.

The Professor had gone on tinkering hopefully, but as he spent less and less time on doctoring, money began to be a problem. He was living on rolled oats and boiled cabbage when the Bank of Dopple—the small town where he had set up his "laboratory"—refused his application for a loan, and the rich young lady he had set his heart on recoiled from his proposal of marriage. No one believed in his genius (as he had once confided to his horrid nephew in Samantha's hearing).

Bitterness at length warped an already ungenerous mind, and the Professor determined to turn the Reducer against his enemies. They would support his research whether they wished or not! His plan was devilishly simple. On the opening day of the county fair, when everyone in Dopple should have been off to the county seat, Kurtz drove his wagon into town, parked in front of the church, climbed in the back, and aimed the Reducer. Church, boarding house, inn, store, bank, and house after house shrank under that baleful eye, to be stowed in the wagon, higgledy-piggledy, and lashed down under a grimy tarpaulin.

"But you see," said Samantha with a sigh, "not everybody *went* to the county fair that year. I was sick, and Mr. Goff had two broken legs, and Miss Umstott had a headache, and. . . . Well, anyhow, there are eight of us. And it's been seven *years*."

Pete had stared. "Eight people, and with all the traveling around you say he's done, he doesn't even know he's *got* you?"

Samantha shrugged impatiently. "They're old houses, with lots of cupboards and inside rooms for hiding, and he's so messy he never notices the food we take. But it's been more dangerous than ever since we came here two days ago so's he could repaint the wagon. It's the barn owls. They think we're mice, and it's been awful. The others are afraid to come out at all for fear they'll be pounced on. They get all puffy and red if they have to run; so I come out for the food and such." She blew her nose on a tiny square of cambric and drew herself up bravely. "I saw you on your way to school, and we decided that next time you came by I should flag you down." She leaned out of sight for a moment, and then hauled up a small red-and-white checked tablecloth on which the word *HELP* had been lettered in bright blue paint from the Professor's worktable.

"But—but what can *I* do?"

Samantha and her friends had already settled about that. In a daze, Pete found himself halfway promised to fetch Constable Dudley and a Mr. Henry Hostetler, who had known Mr. Goff in his unshrunken state. Tomorrow, Samantha insisted. But Pete would not go more than halfway. "I'll think it over," he hedged. Just then the sound of horses coming up the road had sent him full speed up through the waist-high weeds and down into the drainage ditch that crossed the hill fields alongside the upper road. In twenty minutes he was safely home and not at all inclined toward fetching the constable on the morrow. Or ever. Constable Dudley had had an earful of MacCubbin tall tales for years, seeing how often he had Trashbin in jail on Saturday nights for "Disturbing the Peace." Petey could hear his horselaugh already. "Haw! Now, if that don't beat a skunk!"

Saturday inched itself by with house chores and field work, but whenever there was a longish lull Pete thought, "I ought to go down and explain to that Samantha about us and the Law." Later it was, "Mebbe I could tell Miss Ample." But that was no good either. She would just smile and ask what book *that* story came from. Since there was really no point in going down to the old Sampson place until he knew what he meant to do, he started in on cleaning out the spring.

The sun had tilted down into the orchard treetops and Trashbin had long since driven off down the hill in his Saturday night togs before the answer hit Pete over the head. It was so simple. "If it was a snake, it would've bit me," he snorted. *If* he hadn't dreamed it all up, all he had to do was take Samantha *with* him to Miss Ample's. Miss Ample could find Mr. Hostetler and decide what to do. It was too late tonight, but he'd go tomorrow, right after Sunday dinner. Or he could leave early for prayer meeting, before Granny.

This debate was cut short by Granny's exclamation from her back-porch rocker. "Merciful heavens, here's your daddy back already, and he's whipping those poor old mules up the hill like he was Jehu in his chariot!"

Petey slipped out into the dusk beside her to watch the wagon rattle up along the bottom of the south field, past the pigpen, and out of sight behind the barn. It reappeared on the other side with a screeching of wheel and axle, a scrambling of hooves, and creaking of harness as Trashbin tooled the mules around the corner and came to a shuddering stop facing the end barn door. Jumping down with his "collecting bag," he cut between the toolshed and outhouse, leaped a flower bed, and came up across the lawn at a loping run, grinning and humming to himself in a high good humor.

"Boy," he said, "if you want to keep your hide in one piece, you hop along down and get that wagon under cover and them mules unharnessed. You rub 'em down smart, and hie yourself back up here on the double!" He peered after Pete's hurrying figure and then smiled blearily at Granny. "We got us a good boy, there, Maw." He hugged his collecting bag—a grimy gunnysack—to his chest, and it clinked suspiciously. "Heck, Ma!" Trashbin grinned delightedly at her frown. "You ain't even said, 'Evening, Son,' and here I brung you a present out from town."

He groped awkwardly in the bag and fished out a small package tied up in smudgy white tissue paper with a flattened blue bow. "I brung something for the boy's birthday, too, seeing as he's been so down in the mouth about stopping school. Better late than never."

Trashbin was so busy looking sentimental and virtuous that he tripped over the threshold of the kitchen door and missed Granny's comment on opening her present. It was a fancy little silver-labeled blue bottle of Evening in Paris perfume, and she said, "Mmph. Very nice, but I reckon I'd better not ask where you came by the cash."

By the time Petey came up from the barn, Trashbin had changed from his town boots to clodhoppers and come down with a much-shrunken gunnysack load under his arm. "Got to take these here bottles down to my collection," he explained. "I got some big plans afoot—things that take a bit of thinking on. So I allow as how I'll bed down in the haymow tonight so's the two of you won't be after waking me up at the crack of dawn. Anybody comes asking after me, you ain't seen me since before suppertime, you hear?" He wouldn't look Granny in the eye, just said "You hear?" once more, and nipped off down to the barn.

"Oh dear, oh dear, oh dear." Granny sighed, dabbing a touch of the perfume behind her ears to make her feel better. "I do hope he's not got himself in another one of his scrapes. He hasn't been so sweet-spoken since that time they got after him for trying to cart off the lampposts in Sorley Summit to sell for scrap. He brought you a birthday present," she added darkly.

"Is that what was in the sack? I kind of thought there was something more than bottles in it, the way he was hugging at it when he come in." Petey shook his head wonderingly, his own problems forgotten. "Where's it at now?"

"Stowed up in his room, I reckon." Granny took up her palm-leaf fan to wave away the mosquitoes that closed in as the dusk deepened toward dark. "Time you were thinking of bed, isn't it, honey?"

"Yes'm."

Petey went up the stairs slowly. The only present his father ever gave him was a bag of peppermint "lozengers" at Christmastime (though one year it was horehound cough drops). Trashbin didn't believe in birthdays. But tonight—somehow—he had come into enough money to put him in a rare generous mood. Somewhere between home and town. The thought became a cold lump in the pit of Petey's stomach. What was there between the farm and town but the old Sampson place?

Quickly, as quiet as a moth, Petey ducked into Trashbin's room. He looked under the socks and bandannas and underwear in the tallboy and then lifted up the edge of the bed skirt. It was there: a bundle rolled up in a piece of old horse blanket. He was half afraid to look.

A few odds and ends spilled out of the roll as he drew it toward him: a length of rusty lightweight chain, a worn razor strop, a claim ticket from Wise's Second-Hand Shop and Loan Co., a familiar-looking padlock . . . and then there it was, a little dusty from the horse blanket, but still gleaming, all maroon and chrome. It was a perfect 1915-model Hudson roadster straight out of one of the miniature garages.

Not long after midnight Pete awoke with a queer ringing in his ears and heard the dogs barking frantically down by the barn. Half asleep, he stumbled to the window to take the screen out and lower the sash against the sound. Only after he was in bed again and in the half-real world at the edge of dreaming did he realize what he had seen; but even as he puzzled over it, he tumbled into sleep. *There had been a man bending over the barn. . . . A man as tall as the old red maple tree in the barnyard, lifting a corner of the roof and laughing.*

Three

THE WELL HAD GONE DRY. GRANNY, UP AT DAWN, thought at first it was only the kitchen pump out of kilter again. The handle clacked noisily up and down. Priming it with water from the kettle didn't help. When she took the big pitcher to the well's outdoor pump beside the back porch, it too only clacked and sighed.

A little frown creased Granny's forehead. "Now, what can ail the contraption?" Even in the driest of summers the well was sweet and true. How could it fail now, after the wettest of springs? Granny didn't puzzle long—the water for coffee and oatmeal should have been on and boiling by now—but went down through the rose arbor to the springhouse.

In the springhouse the wide, cemented stone basin under the low mossy roof was, as always, brimful. But the little overflow stream that should have trickled among the day lilies and trillium and down past the chicken coop was dry as bone. The stone spout where water poured into the basin was dry too, and the milk cans and applejack jugs sitting in the water were not chilly to the touch, only cool.

Granny dipped her pitcher carefully, trying all the while to puzzle it out, but she could not. There was a worried hunch to her shoulders as she hurried back to her kitchen.

Petey hovered sleepily over the stove. He looked as if he thought to find the oatmeal by staring at the spot where it ought to be. Granny smiled.

"I'll toast you a slice of bread real quick," she said. "It'll hold you down till the porridge is ready. And I reckon I'll make do with milk 'stead of coffee." She told him about the well and the spring.

"Not a trickle?" Petey's yawn became a groan. "You mean I got to tote water up from the creek to fill *all* them barnyard troughs so's they aren't drunk dry?"

"*Have* to and all *those*," said Granny disapprovingly. "Yes, I'm afraid so. We'll have to miss morning church and just go to prayer meeting tonight. If the water doesn't come back, we'll have to get Dan Binns up to dig us a new well, and where the money's to come from for *that*, I don't know. The whole thing's downright peculiar."

She carefully sifted the oatmeal into the now boiling water. "I could understand it if there were coal mines under us, like up north a ways, high on the ridge. Their tunnels can cut across underground seep-ways, I hear tell, and drain off water from folk downhill. But there's no such a thing hereabouts. I just can't understand it. Still. . . ." She dusted her hands off briskly.

"Worry's no help. The water may come back as quick as it went off. We'll see to the reg'lar chores and then take a couple spades down to the blackberry patch 'fore you set to toting water buckets. There's a lot of nasty dock weeds got in amongst the bushes and need digging out." She stirred briskly. "Here now, you bring the bowls, dearie, and then fetch another pitcher of milk up from the springhouse."

After the milking and feeding the stock, Petey and Mrs. MacCubbin took the shortcut to the berry patch, across the south field between two rows of young potato plants. Midway, Petey slowed. As Granny came up behind, he cocked his head a little and said, "Hark at that!"

Granny heard it too. "I declare! The well's gone dry, but the creek must be running fit to bust its banks if we can hear it clear up here."

Further on the sound of rushing water grew even louder, but other things than that were queer. Potato plants tilted tipsily, and what had been well-groomed rows staggered muddily on for several yards and toppled out of sight.

"Mercy me!" Granny exclaimed. It was all she could say. "Mercy me!"

Down through the field, some yards from its far edge, flowed a strange creek. It apparently welled up at the top of the field, where fence and turf and earth were rucked up in a drunken heap. It was two or three feet deep and must have been twelve feet across.

"I do declare!" Granny sat down weakly among the potatoes. "Whatever can have happened?"

Petey shook his head, bewildered. "The creek," he

said at last. "Mebbe the creek's dammed up above the north field and come past the orchard down this way? I bet that old deadfall tree fell acrost it. Branches and such could snag up against it and. . . ." At Granny's doubtful look, he trailed off.

"T'ain't likely." She hoisted herself up with the help of the small shovel. "This here's twice the water Old Way Creek ever held. But we'll get to the bottom of it straight out. We'll just follow up along and *see*."

And Petey was wrong.

The new creek welled up out of nowhere, rising in a muddy rush among the mangels growing at the top of the field. Skirting above it, Granny came down along the other side. Nothing. It made no sense, but there it was. With a deepening frown, the old lady headed on across the field to the shade of the old maples along the rail fence that separated field and pasture. The blackberry patch was a messy tangle along the fence-row in an open stretch where chestnut trees had grown before the blight.

But Granny and Petey didn't get as far down the fence as the berry patch. Coming out of the sun's dazzle into the shade, they saw that the pasture beyond the trees was gone.

Where it had been there was now a wide, sloping plain of raw yellow earth, littered with shards of sandstone. Here and there, yellow boulders bulked up with oddly sheared-off tops. Only the faraway trees glowing green in the sunlight reassured Petey that he had not stumbled onto one of Mr. Verne's lunar landscapes in a dream. . . . But the trees looked somehow wrong, and the naked slope in between was certainly so. He pinched himself—hard—but it didn't change a thing. A horrid suspicion crept into his mind. One old, dry spring, one new and gigantic spring, a hillside mysteriously bare—perhaps they weren't all that was out of kilter. What if last night's glimpse of a man peering under the roof of the barn *hadn't* been a dream? That Reducer-thing? What if it had been Professor Lilliput, and he had. . . . Petey thrust the awful thought away resolutely.

Granny, even in a bewildered flutter, missed nothing. She saw the sick, closed-up look on Petey's face, the scowling squint he had when he was doing sums in his head, and his unhappy glance back over his shoulder to the barn.

"What is it, child?" Red-faced, she fanned herself with a handful of maple leaves. "Best tell me now, before I decide 'tween sunstroke and brain fever."

"It's nothin'. Leastways, I don't see how it could . . ." Petey was as pale as midwinter. "I thought there was this—this sort of fairy tale I dreamed up. Only mebbe it wasn't me after all. It could be Paw's stuck his big foot right in the middle of something nasty."

He took a deep breath. "I—I reckon we'd best go talk to Paw."

"*Shrunk?* The whole dad-burned farm? It ain't so," whimpered a stubbly wild-eyed Trashbin. "It ain't so, and I ain't gonter listen to such a pack of nonsense. Pastures and woods don't just up and walk away, neither. Now you get on out of here and leave me be. I got nothing to say to the two of you." Trashbin burrowed deeper into the hay, sneezing miserably.

"I ain't a well man." His voice came out as a muffled snuffle. "Anybody who'd sneak in where he hadn't ought to be to open a birthday present, and then say his daddy . . . *thieved* it, well, he don't *deserve* no birthday present. I'm gonter take it back where I got it. That's what I'm gonter do." The hay shivered.

Granny, perched near the top of the loft ladder, snorted. "You just do that, Donalbain MacCubbin. But first you come right out of there. You know how hay swells up your eyes. I don't want to be doctoring you when the whole farm's turned topsy-turvy."

Mouselike, the miserable, red-eyed, whiskery face reappeared in a little window his fingers scrabbled in the mound of hay. "Maw? You ain't got a bit of wild mint up to the kitchen you could brew some tea of, have you? I—I *ain't* a well man. If you'll just tell me all them things about the woods bein' scalped off is a leg-pull, mebbe I'll come down arter a whiles."

"You looky here, Paw," put in Petey—bravely, now that Trashbin's roar was tamed to a snuffle. "I *know* where you got that little car, because I seen it there. *Saw* it there," he amended at Granny's frown. "And by what I hear, that Professor Lilliput's such a mean old twister it wouldn't do a lick of good to take it back even if you could. So you can tell us just what happened. It won't make no never mind now."

Inching a bit further out, Trashbin said, with a sort of weak bravado, "Well, if he ain't took it out of my hide by now, I reckon mebbe I'll keep it just to spite the feller. Them quack doctors is all cheats anyhow. You might say I served him with a spoonful of his own sauce." Recovering, he told his tale almost boastfully.

He had, he said, been scouting the old Sampson place with an eye to picking up another bit or two of hardware that might be lying around getting rusty, and his eye had been caught by the new padlocks on the barn. The little east door, he knew, had always been blocked tight from inside by a great pile of lumber oddments and discarded mildewed furniture. A shiny new padlock was wasted there—and easy enough to fiddle open with a bit of wire. Order a new key from Hopwood's Hardware, and a good lock like that might fetch two dollars.

One padlock led to another, and the second door was clear. "Blessed if it wasn't better'n a peep show! All them bitty houses. I knew it weren't like sneaking old hardware, but they was so wonderful, cunning made with all their bitty porch lamps and knockers and windows with shutters that my fingers fair itched to hoist one of 'em up and run fer it. But I thought me, 'MacCubbin, them things must weigh thirty–forty pounds. You just take that little car and shut the little shed door arter it, so's it ain't missed!' And that's all I done." With the hay like a halo in his hair, he managed to look the picture of misjudged virtue.

Petey was unimpressed. "So the Professor passed you and the mules between Inkle's Springs and town. Soon as he missed it, he'd know it was you took it and take off after you."

"I wonder. Might there have been something he missed quicker?" asked Granny shrewdly. "That's it, eh? You got that weasely look again, my boy. What was it?"

Trashbin slumped back onto the haypile. "Awright,"

he mumbled sullenly. "There was this here gold watch. It was in a valise under a heap of fancy shirts, and arter I saw it, it kind of—well, slid into my pocket. Afore I could think what a awful thing I done, I was drivin' down to the main road, and there come your prissy P-Professor."

Trashbin wrung his hands nervously. "Soon as I got in town, I pawned it. Old Man Wise give me twenty-five dollars on it. And that's the whole of it, honest Injun. Except. . . ." He faltered. ". . . excepting, there was this dream I had. . . ."

Petey shivered as he too remembered.

"The roof. He picked up a corner of the roof and had a look in at you."

Trashbin blanched. "It—it weren't a dream, then, were it? You'd best tell me the worst, boy. The whole caboodle."

Four

WILHELM KURTZ—OR PROFESSOR LILLIPUT, AS HE HAD styled himself in the years after he had reduced the town of Dopple and turned it into a traveling exhibit —had detected the theft within minutes of his return and set out in wrathful pursuit. His hillbilly thief was a well-known local character and would not be hard to locate. The gold repeater watch was certain to be found at the local pawnshop. He had only to report the theft and Constable Dudley would see it restored to him. Unfortunately, there was the matter of the miniature car. It might not do after all to set the constable after the thief.

The Professor pulled up his horse to let it graze along the grassy verge. No, it would not do at all. If the constable should wish to visit the scene of the crime. . . . Badly lit as the inside of the wagon was, there was still the danger that a sharp-eyed and curious visitor might see too clearly how finely detailed the houses were. Here and there such deliberately out-of-proportion touches as a stumpy front-porch rocker obviously made from matchsticks, a china Alsatian watchdog, or a slightly oversize brass candlestick had been added in an attempt to give the former town of Dopple a more convincingly handmade and doll's house-ish look, but with doubtful success. It would be better to have a permanent museum instead of the wagon display, with the houses arranged on long wide tables that held visitors beyond arm's length. "One day. . . ." The Professor always ground his teeth when he thought of the museum. It seemed no nearer as the years passed. "All it takes is a little capital," he muttered.

And caution. Constable Dudley was a rumpled, amiable, sleepy sort of man, but sharp as a tack nonetheless. Sending him up the ridge after MacCubbin once the watch was recovered from the pawnshop might mean the recovery of the valuable little roadster, but it could mean exposure as well. The constable, who putted around on an old motorbike and read *Motor World* while he lunched at Dobbie's Diner, was bound to be intrigued by the realistic details on the little Hudson. The temptation to insert the crank handle under the bumper and give it a turn or two could be fatal, for if there were gas in the tank, the game was up. One cough, sputter, or quiver—whether the engine started or not—could attract a lot of very dangerous curiosity.

Then there was MacCubbin himself. A shifty sort of buzzard, lazy and a braggart, he was sharp too. Maybe sharp enough to sniff out the history of the Marvelous Museum of Miniatures and try his hand at blackmail.

That would be disastrous. There was too much work yet to be done on the Reducer: refinements to be made, principles to be mastered, and not a penny to be spared. If only he had the protection of a patent, he could chuck the museum and its risks and enlist the backing of serious investors.

Unfortunately, the workings of the machine were not perfectly clear. There was great risk that in taking it apart one might not get it together again. Three times the Professor's drawings had come back from the Patent Office in Washington with polite notes to the effect that "the intended function of this invention remains obscure, *viz.*, in its present stage of development it is unlikely that it does anything. We prefer to await your presentation of a practical model and more detailed wiring diagrams before processing your application." Year after year, delay and frustration. There was a fortune in the Reducer, but only if he could master it. And now this new threat. . . .

The solution was, of course, at hand. The Reducer itself. What could be more simple?

A careful question or two in town established that the MacCubbins kept pretty much to themselves and that callers were not welcomed up on the ridge. Trashbin saw to that. The Professor returned to the old Sampson barn and set to work.

Having rented the barn, the Professor had no qualms about commandeering a cart discovered behind a heap of junk. Once the tarpaulin-covered Reducer was trundled up a plank onto the cart and securely lashed down, he took time for a bite of supper. Then he loaded up his Novo Portable Generator, harnessed the horses to the groaning cart, and set off up the ridge road.

Barring a rough stretch of road in the steep gully below the MacCubbin place—and the sharp bend at the top of the gully where the Reducer threatened to tip into the creek—all went well. When Trashbin tooled past half an hour later, lashing the wheezing mules the last hundred yards, horses, wagon, Reducer, and Professor were hidden in the gloom under the oak trees down from the barn. For half an hour they waited quietly.

At ten o'clock the Professor reached absently for the watch chain that was not there. "Drat the fellow! Still, it's the last watch he'll steal. We'll see to that, my pretty." He climbed onto the back of the cart, patted the top of the Reducer affectionately, and bent close to examine its dials by the light of a match. "Let us see. For maximum minification . . . so!" He flipped the switch marked MINIFY and then, lighting another match, adjusted several of the black knobs clustering like warts here and there on the Reducer's sides. "Wide angle exposure—ha! We'll try for the whole farm, eh, my little love? Good, good. Maximum depth of field— hum. Lateral penetration—*ouch!*" He dropped the match and struck another. "To the Nth power. There, that ought to do it."

The palms of his hands were moist with excitement. He wiped them carefully on a large red silk handkerchief before making the last fine adjustment, aiming the Reducer's piglike snout up across the sloping barnyard to the trim log farmhouse. The square of yellow light that spilled from one window made an excellent target. The Professor rubbed his hands.

"Generator—*on*." The new automatic starter set the generator's gasoline engine going with a brisk clatter. "Good, good. Power building nicely," murmured the Professor. As the chatter blurred into a rising hum, he put a finger to the main switch.

"Now!"

The night shivered. Like a still pond at the wind's first touch, the farm trembled against the shores of

woods and sky. And then it was gone, peeled away as if it had been only a painted patch on the night. It went with a soft deep THWUU*UMP*PH! that bent the tops of the untouched trees and sucked the Professor's breath half away.

It was not precisely gone. Not utterly. When Wilhelm Kurtz, alias Professor Lilliput, recovered from his fright, he crept out across a naked field of stones toward the little patch of scrub that huddled in its middle. There, ancient trees that minutes before had towered eighty or a hundred feet and more were matted into a hedge no higher than ten feet at its tallest.

Forcing his way between two oaks, he set one foot gingerly before the other along a road no wider than a woodland path. Reaching the barn, he lifted a corner of the roof by its drooping eave and grinned in at the cowering Trashbin.

Five

"I DO DECLARE!" GRANNY SAT, PALE BUT VERY STRAIGHT, on a bale of hay, and shook her head. "It's a mite much to take in all at once."

"You take it in," quavered Trashbin, suddenly mulish. "I say it was no such a thing." Disbelief was easier with a good solid story to disbelieve in.

Petey would have argued, but Granny was already thinking of what must be done. First off, word must be got to Judge Hesselbein. Granny firmly believed in starting at the top, and she knew the Judge to nod to, from church. A note. She must get a note to him somehow. Granny retied the strings of her sunbonnet.

"We've no time to waste on quibbles, my dears. We need help, and right quick. Before that dreadful man can leave Mosstown."

"He can't leave 'fore next Saturday," Petey offered. He squinted, trying to remember the Professor's poster. "Next Saturday, noon to nine, he's got to be there."

Old Mrs. MacCubbin frowned. "There's naught to stop the villain leaving whenever he fancies, child. Unless he means us more mischief, it's my guess he'll be off soon's he can pack up. Today or tomorrow."

She stood, briskly dusting hay from her calico skirts. "You come along out of there, Donalbain, and go stick your head under the pump. Petey and I'll have the mules harnessed in two shakes." She eyed the scarecrow face under its halo of hay and added sourly, "You'd best take an extry minute and shave yourself, or folks are like to take you for some whiskery rodent."

Trashbin bridled, but then sank back against the haystack. "There ain't no call fer flingin' insults at me, Maw," he quavered. "I ain't well. I ain't well enough t'drag up to my own bed, let alone go harin' into town."

He sniffled, avoiding their eyes. "All that guff about a Shrinking Machine—it's only another o' your tricks to flimflam me into drivin' the two of you into church. A pretty fool I'd look too, drivin' down the road, keepin' an eye peeled fer folks seventy feet tall." He shivered, though his face was flushed and sweaty under the dust and grime. "I ain't gonter move," he whined. "I'm a ill man."

Granny snorted.

"There's no denying that," she said, in a tone that set Trashbin puzzling over what he had said. She sighed. "Anyhow, I reckon the way you go, you'd break an axle driving acrost that monstrous stony field like it was the Lincoln Highway. And as fer riding, any mule with a scrap of sense'd rather have a sack of meal on its back." She turned. "Petey, child, I reckon it's up to you."

The wagon, as Petey saw once he and Jenny the mule were on their way, would never have made it. Great boulders and lesser stones did indeed litter the naked brown and yellow wasteland beyond the potato field fence, but far worse was the clayey yellow soil itself. The sun would soon enough bake its surface to a hard crust, but at midmorning it was still moist.

At first Jenny's hooves sank in to the fetlock, coming out again with a hollow sucking *phlop*!, and soon she was picking her way along like an old lady in too-high heels, as the clay stuck fast. A dozen times Petey dismounted to scrape the balled clay from her hooves with a rock shard. The struggle to remount was considerable, for Jenny was not only tall in the shoulder, but her roached mane offered no handhold.

"Phew! Don't I wish you was a camel!" panted Petey, red-faced from jumping up and slipping down. In *A Geography of the Whole World* there were pictures of Arabs daintily stepping aboard thoughtfully kneeling camels. Neither Jenny's knees nor her temper were so accommodating. Wearying of Petey's determined attacks on her left flank, she took to stepping neatly out of range just as he launched himself.

In the end Petey took his good town boots off, tied them together by their laces so as to hang them around his neck, and led the mule fifty yards or so to a great flat rock some three feet high. With the rock for a step, he mounted easily. He took care to make the next stop beside a similarly convenient mounting block.

They had gone perhaps half a mile—or what seemed so—and the wasteland still stretched before them. Nothing about the stripped land was familiar. It rolled endlessly, like one of Mr. Verne's imaginary moonscapes, from under the distant towering trees.

Only gradually did a fringe of brighter green appear between the muddy yellow and that high motionless backdrop of trees and grow against that darker green until it touched the summer-bright sky. The edge of the woods at last!

Petey let out a long breath. The dread that had settled on him in the middle of the yellow waste evaporated. The trees were no illusion. The rest of the world was still there! There would be shade, and a chance to rest out of the midday sun. Jenny's reddish coat was black with sweat. Petey's shirt stuck to his back, and his backside stuck to Jenny.

But—the nearer they came, the odder the forest looked. It stood—*seemed* to stand—atop a steeply curving rise. And if the farm *had* been shrunk by the Professor's diabolical machine, oughtn't the surrounding woods seem to tower about twelve times higher than before? If you were suddenly five and a half inches tall, an eighty-foot tree should look . . . near a thousand feet tall! Further off, the darker ones had looked as if they might be, but not these.

The air shimmered with the heat, and Petey imagined that the woods themselves swayed, shifting lightly back and forth. Their rustling sigh rose and fell in the heavy air as loudly as a rising wind in a maple grove. Petey pulled out his shirttail to wipe the sweat from his forehead, then shaded his eyes with his hand, and squinted.

It wasn't the woods at all. It was straight out of the *Geography*'s chapter on "India, Burma, and the Straits Settlements": a dense, towering, impenetrable forest of bamboo.

Jenny backed up. She laid her long ears back, rolled her eyes, and snuffled and snorted her bafflement. Petey did a bit of sniffing himself. Badly frightened and considerably confused, he still kept his head. The pungent, sweet, familiar smell that hung in the shimmering air at least was real and known, an invisible touchstone. And *strong*. He felt that if only he could get hold of what it was, everything would make sense. He hitched up his shirttail again to wipe the sweat from his eyes— and the moment he closed them, the smell and that busy rustling sound echoed in his remembering . . . *himself, hiding from Trashbin in one of his ugly I'll-thrash-*YOU *moods, hiding beyond the berry brambles, stretched out flat in the knee-deep grass.*

Grass, not bamboo! Petey stared. It was one thing to guess what fate had befallen the farm, to know that you were just over five inches tall, and quite another to see and feel it. Grass!

Jenny, confused about everything but the smell of her own pasture, abruptly stepped out with a sharp snort that meant, "About *time* for a bite to eat."

Thirty yards away, she slowed to a bewildered walk. The slopes curved up sharply, steepening almost into a cliff. Along its rim the Grass Wood rustled. Jenny swung her head this way and that through the overpowering scent of rich green hay as if to say, "Where did it *go?*" In her distraction she did not see the ladybug, swinging overhead on one bent green blade, or the two ants as long as Petey's hand, who were exploring, head-first, the dark earth slope where it met the rising yellow plain.

Professor Lilliput's Reducer had been powerful enough to shrink the farm to a ninth of an acre smack in the middle of the sixteen acres it had been, but fortunately it had penetrated at its deepest only some two feet below the surface. To Petey those two feet seemed twenty-four, but it could have been much worse. As it was, a passerby would have seen only a wide shallow depression with a goodish clump of scrub trees—the old trees ringing the farm—at its center.

Pete turned Jenny east along the foot of this grass-topped mesa toward the bottom of her old pasture. He hoped, with luck, to be able to scramble up to the road where it skirted the meadow. The going would be easier and safer, once they reached the leaf-mold carpet of the woods. Time enough to worry about a way through the grassy meadow above the Sampson barn when they came to it.

Unfortunately, they were never to come to it. At the same moment that Petey sighted a break ahead in the wall of tall grass, a young snake not many hours out of the egg came slithering down the slope. Jenny, see-ing (as she thought) a three-foot-long viper in brilliant green, gave a honking scream as she wheeled in panic and stumbled to her knees. Petey was pitched over her head.

"Jenny, gal? Ho, Jen! It's only a grass snake, you fool mule!" Petey picked himself up gingerly. He had landed heavily on his shoulder, but it still seemed to be in working order. Between the sun's glare and a dizzy wobble that had got into the scenery, it was sev-eral moments before he spied the mule. She stood about ten yards away, plastered against one of the great boulders, trembling, head up, one forefoot held gin-gerly in the air. The dark-eyed young snake lay frozen

(44)

a few feet behind Petey in earnest imitation of a blade of grass.

"Sh-shoo!" managed Petey, with a shaky laugh. "Go chase yourself a horsefly. G'wan!" He rattled a pebble toward it, and it fled along the bank, a green flash, gone in a wink.

"It's all right, old girl." Petey talked his way over to the frightened mule. "No need to get spooked at a bitty grass snake. It just *looked* big." He considered. "Well, no, it *was* big, I suppose. But not big enough to wish us harm. You ain't no mosquito." He rubbed Jenny's flank reassuringly and moved in close to her shoulder.

"Did yourself a hurt, didn't you? Just let's feel, old lady." He ran a hand down her near foreleg, and she winced away. A bad sprain, he guessed.

"Well, we'd never made it to town any old how," Pete sighed. He sat on a rock and untied the bandanna-wrapped packet of sandwiches that had hung from one of his belt loops. "It's past noon and we've got exactly nowheres."

Jenny leaned in the skimpy shade of her boulder. When the sandwiches were finished, Petey led her the long limping way home.

"You're entirely right." Granny sighed, put down the stub of pencil, and took off her reading spectacles. "Mosstown's four miles—four *real* miles—away. You say that little girl was 'bout five inches tall, and this little car looks near a foot long, so an inch to a foot must be about right. That makes four miles as good as forty-eight now!"

Petey held the little Hudson car and turned the steering wheel with his thumb and forefinger, watching fascinated as the little roadster's front wheels turned and straightened. "It looks the same as before, so it's been double-shrunk," he marveled. "It may *look* a foot long still, but it ain't more'n one *inch* long in real inches."

Granny paid him no mind. "Forty-eight miles. Hmm. I s'pose Jack could do it easy enough between sunrise and dusk if he wasn't in one of his ornery takings." Jack was only a hand taller than Jenny, but with his thick shoulders and rolling eye, he looked the biggest, meanest mule in Creation.

"He don't much like anybody up on his back," Petey offered doubtfully.

Granny pushed up from her rocker and headed for the cupboard under the stairs. "There's that old canvas shooting vest," she announced. "It's got good big pockets to hold you two-three bottles of ginger beer to wash down sandwiches and cake. I'll bake an angel food cake tonight. You'd like a nice piece of that to take along tomorrow, wouldn't you?" Her voice echoed dimly from the closet where she had her head in the old canvas-covered trunk.

"Yes'm," said Petey. But he was thinking of ornery Jack and wondering whether staying five-inches-and-a-bit tall for a while would be so very awful after all.

Jack, almost always contrary until midday, this morning did a little dance in his stall and leaned out to give Petey a damply affectionate blow down his collar and a hearty nudge to the breastbone. Far from objecting to either bridle or rider, he did not even boggle

at the creaky antique saddle Petey eased onto his back in a cautious experiment. Whether it was genuine good humor or simply the urge to be well away from his hobbling and fretful Jenny, at a little past six he struck out at a smart trot with Petey enjoying the security of a saddle horn to cling to.

The game pockets of the canvas hunter's vest bulged with lunch and supper and pinned to the inside breast pocket were letters to Judge Hesselbein and Parson Knott. They made a thick wad, for Granny, realizing that yesterday's notepaper letters would be impossibly small for their full-size readers, had copied them onto the largest and least rumpled sheets of her collection of used butcher paper, writing in a large well-rounded hand with Trashbin's lucky rabbit's foot for a make-shift ink brush.

There was also a note to Miss Ample, asking whether she would mind putting Petey up until the authorities had set things right. "I shall rest Easy," said the firm, old-fashioned script, "knowing that Peter sleeps under a Roof, and trust that you will see him safe from your Catts."

Petey and Jack gained the road without mishap, climbing to the rim of the wasteland where an earthfall had made a sort of ramp. The early sun touched the mountain-high treetops ahead, but the rutted road still held the night chill and was damp with dew. Along the shadowy downhill side of the eerily wide road marched oaks and beeches so tall that looking up gave Petey a crick in his neck.

As sunshine stirred the woods to life, poking fingers into spiders' webs and chipmunk holes, Petey went more carefully. They kept to the road, for after yesterday Petey felt there might be too many surprises underfoot in the woods.

Jack's good humor wavered a little as he puzzled over a route that smelled right but looked uncommonly wrong. Having had an elegant breakfast of cracked barley, he had not noticed the lack of sweet green grass for roadside snacks. It was the first chipmunk that stopped him dead. It sat up, staring at him eye-to-eye for a long frozen moment before it broke and fled. For the full five minutes it took poor Jack to decide between fright and indignation, he could not be budged. Petey drummed his barrel sides with his

boots and yelled, "Gee-*yup!*" and "C'mon, you jack-ass!" but Jack only swiveled his ears and rolled his eyes.

Finally, unexpectedly, Jack did move, delicately footing his way onto the dusty crest between the ruts where the going was easier than down among the wheel-worn boulders. Petey could scarcely believe his luck. Ornery Jack! Maybe he was *so* ornery that if he felt good, the rest of the world could *be* out of whack and bad cess to it. It made no never mind to Jack!

A short distance above the Sampson barn Petey, more wary than Jack, turned the mule out of the road lest the Professor catch sight of them. A long-forgotten footpath straggled through the grass along the pasture fence, and Petey guessed that it tilted down toward White Oak Creek. He was not sure. The familiar fields were as strange as if they had been the forests of darkest Africa. Only at the deepening sound ahead, a rushing clatter, did he hurry the mule with a kick in the ribs. The worst was over! There was a path along the creek all the way into Mosstown, overgrown in places, but a path.

Coming out of the tall grass, they stepped into the cool, damp shade where the creek threaded along the borders of the wood. And stopped.

A weasel crouched on the far bank, drinking. He raised his head and, whiskers dripping, fixed a velvet black eye on the unfortunate travelers. It was the thoughtful and appreciative look of a polite creature unexpectedly invited to lunch.

Six

"PETEY! PETEY DEAR, WAKE UP. CHILD, IF YOU'RE BAD hurt, I shall never forgive myself. Petey!" Granny shook his shoulder and then went back to patting his forehead with a cold wet cloth. The drips ran into his ear and down his neck. He could not see—and then found his eyes were shut. Opening them helped very little.

"Bless your heart!" Granny's warm, papery lips brushed his cheek with a thankful kiss. "Now, set up easy. You've a bump on your forehead the size of a goose egg. Did that blamed mule tip you off and light out somewheres on his own? I feared as much. It come over me at lunchtime. 'Petey's in trouble,' I said to myself, and I couldn't put it out of my head. Next thing I knew, I'd fetched the shotgun and packed a supper. A good thing, too. You'd have caught your death of pneumonia here on the damp ground."

Petey squinted painfully. "How's come it's so dark?"

Granny laughed. "The sun set near half an hour ago, child. My old feet took their time getting me here, and I just hope they get me back 'fore they blister clean off."

"Jack!" Petey scrambled to his feet, pale and a little dizzy. "Granny, you didn't see Jack? He . . . he didn't go along home?"

Granny pulled an extra shawl out of her basket and draped it around his shoulders. "I've not seen hide nor hair of him, dearie. What happened? Here, you come along and we'll find somewheres dry and warm. We'll have us some ham and chutney and cold tea and angel cake while you tell me about it. Sampson's barn is empty. We'll go there."

Sampson's barn being empty was worse luck for the MacCubbins than the horrid accident that certainly had overtaken Jack. It meant no Professor. The barn loomed huge in the dusk, a dark mountain against a sky streaked with the last pink wisps of sunset.

Petey stuck his head in at the crack between the two huge leaves of the main door. "I can't see nothing, Gran," he whispered. "You *sure* they're gone?"

"Yes. I took a peek while it was still light. I thought that Professor—Kurtz or Lilliput or whatever his name is—might've caught you and shut you up in a jam jar." Granny nudged him in ahead of her.

She set down her basket just inside the door and produced from it a faded tea towel for a tablecloth, half a loaf of wheaten bread, a square of cheese, sliced ham and chutney and cake, a bottle of tea, and a battered lantern bearing the legend "Property B. & O. R.R." around its base. Lifting the glass chimney, she struck a match on a stone and touched it to the wick.

"Come along, child. Tuck some supper in you so's we can get along home. The sooner I'm there the better I'll like it. I don't fancy being a midnight snack for any nasty varmint."

"Me neither." Petey shivered, thinking of poor Jack.

Only after two thick ham sandwiches and a large slab of cake washed down with tea did Petey take a look around the barn—or as much of it as the lantern's smoky glow showed. Beyond the bright pool at their feet light only faintly touched the great door and nearby wall, but Petey, peering upward, suddenly stiffened. The rough circle of a knothole gaped darkly at the light's dim edge.

The last swallow of cake went down in one lump. It was the knothole where that little Samantha had sat, just by his shoulder. *Was I really that big?* It was almost past imagining.

Granny followed his gaze. "What is it? That scrap of white flapping up yonder? Just a bit of paper, ain't it?" She flapped the crumbs from the teacloth, rolled the empty bottle in it, and stowed them in the basket.

Samantha had apparently reached her perch by climbing a stack of old drainage tiles. Once at the top, Petey found a folded wad of paper wedged in the crack between the knothole board and that next to it. He dragged it free and dropped it to the floor below, then clambered back down.

Granny and Petey spread the crackling sheet of paper out between them on the barn floor. It was as thick as tagboard. The penciled message was a faint and hasty scrawl: *Something has happent,* it said.

> *I don't know what. The Prof has*
> *stuck the extra house in the barn*
> *loft and packt up the rest. I can*
> *rite this as he has rode into the*
> *Town to collect his posters.*
> *Mister Goff saw on the Prof's*
> *calendar where we go Next, so please*
> *can you still help us?*

The writing grew smaller and smaller as the space on the paper shrank and Samantha's agitation increased.

> *. . . It is to Hoxy and Billboro, then*
> *Boswell and someplace called Sorely*
> *Summat and in July to Bedford and*
> *Lake Meander and Pokonomee if that*
> *is how you spell it. Can you set*
> *the Sheriff on us? We will be*
> *eturnally in your Debt (that is*
> *what Miss Umstott says. I would*
> *say Hoorah).*
>
> *Your freind, Samantha*

And that was that. The Professor had got away, and there was little hope that he would keep to his original schedule now.

Petey took up the shotgun and lantern and Granny her basket. They left the note weighted down on a flat stone outside the barn, in case of passersby. But the hope that it might eventually fall into Constable Dudley's hands, or the sheriff's, was not one to count on.

"Do just as much good to put it in a bottle and send it down the creek," sighed Granny. "Well. Tomorrow. Tomorrow we'll decide what to do. We'll rest us up and have a think."

Out of consideration for Granny's feet, they broke the homeward journey with frequent rest stops, but the old lady refused to be tempted by suggestions of a campfire and a mossy bed. The moon was rising when the kerosene lantern burned out at last, and soon the broad stony roadway was almost as bright as day. Petey kept the shotgun at the ready for fear of night creatures, but they saw none. After the lantern winked out, even the fat, blundering moths disappeared.

The chill before dawn pinched the travelers awake when they were tempted to sit down and sleep in the stony wasteland, and so the first light, fingering through the trees, saw them home at last. The thick fringe of oaks and maples shut out the giant world. Petey scuffed through the grass—beautiful grass scarcely high enough to dampen his trouser bottoms—and would have rolled in it if he had not been too weary to get up again.

"It's tomorrow," he said, his smile slipping into a yawn. "And I'm goin' to sleep till *tomorrow*-tomorrow. Mebbe then—"

Granny plucked him sharply by the sleeve. "Hush, child!" Her thin little hand trembled on his wrist. "Hush up and listen." All sleepiness gone, she cocked her head, birdlike, listening.

It was a wonder they had not heard the uproar before. Dogs barked, cows lowed, the bull bellowed. Someone—Jenny or the bull—beat on a stall wall like a drum, and the hens squawked hoarsely in a mad dawn chorus.

And little wonder. Two of the six sheep in the barnyard fold were dead of bee stings, and the other four cowered in a corner, bloody and exhausted from the struggle to climb over each other and out. The dusty chicken yard was drowned in mud. The water troughs were bone dry—hence the hoarsely bellowing stock. In the orchard, three huge, beady-eyed, purple-sheened starlings screamed to each other above the hubbub in between gobbles of tiny green apples.

"Land sakes!" Granny sat down weakly on the bench by the rose arbor to survey the shambles.

Petey was fit to be tied. He sputtered helplessly and kicked out at the fat terrier Nipper to stop his howling. In a minute he had regained his temper and was just plain angry. Snatching the extra shotgun shells from Granny's basket, he slipped up through the side garden in a crouching run. As far as the front porch there were the hydrangeas and currant bushes for cover. Then it was a short dash to the orchard fence.

Bang!

The double-barreled shotgun blast sent the starlings racketing off in alarm. They would be back, though, and what then?

Granny had hurried in search of Trashbin. He was not in the barn. Petey came with the shotgun, and they searched the outbuildings, thinking terrible thoughts about weasels and foxes, their worry mixed with impatience. There was work to be done. There was water to be carried, and the sheep must be folded in the barn before they dithered into total collapse.

Trashbin had apparently made his way from the barn to the house before nightfall. Finding Granny gone, he had invited in most of the dogs for company. The kitchen was full of scruffy hound dogs—Buster and Muggs, Spot and Cissy, Meeny, Miney and Mo—all barking. Buster scrabbled at the back door, which was, of course, bolted from the inside. Mo stood in Granny's kitchen sink, yapping miserably at the window, and when Petey pried it open to climb in, he was half-smothered with doggy kisses.

Trashbin was under the kitchen table. Still hay-strewn and unshaven, he whuffled and snored contentedly, curled around a table leg. Granny's medicinal brandy bottle stood empty beside him. Petey sighed and unbolted the door.

"Now, if that don't beat all." Granny was disgusted. As she shooed out the dogs, her foot clinked against a second bottle. The label said "Doctor Bayliss' Elixir," and it too was empty. "Why, it's my arthritis medicine! Whatever's he been drinking that for?"

She set the bottle in the sink. "Dear me! Listen to those cows. There won't be much milk or eggs today with all this carrying-on." She took off her bonnet, unpinned her shawl, and rolled up her sleeves.

"Well, now. Seems we have to put off worrying how to get the place put back to its rightful size and concentrate us on seeing there's a MacCubbin farm left to *put* right."

Petey nodded glumly. "Anyhow, we know where old Lilliput-Kurtz might be off to." Then he brightened a bit. "Maybe if I could rig some kind of boat, there's the creek. Still. . . ."

"Still—" Granny briskly shoved him ahead of her with a grim, "First things first."

Seven

FIRST AMONG THE FIRST THINGS, TRASHBIN WAS AWAKened and persuaded into the parlor and onto the sofa, where a plush pillow was put under his head and a knitted afghan tucked around him. Then Petey and Granny tackled the chores and cleanup—or, rather, made a start at tackling them. The cleanup went on for days, during which time Trashbin betook himself upstairs to bed with a "consumptive cold." And chores, of course, go on forever.

A dozen or so trips with buckets out across the potato field to the new stream and the thirsty animals were satisfied—for the moment. The new stream, as far as could be figured, arose in the neighborhood—that is, *under* the *former* neighborhood of the old farmhouse spring. The farm had simply shrunk away from it, so that the old stone springhouse now sat atop a perfectly dry spot. The mucky mess in the chicken run, Granny speculated, *might* be caused by the tiny leak of a spring that had previously been too small to do anything but make a squishy spot in the lawn near the nasturtium bed. If it was large enough now to turn the dusty chicken yard into a pig wallow, it might be turned to better use. Just as a stopgap, of course. Until the farm was set right again.

Wearing an old much-patched pair of fisherman's waders, Petey, under Granny's direction, dug a deep hole in the upper south corner of the chicken yard. In half an hour it had filled itself to the top. The overflow trickled down a muddy channel, under the henhouse steps, and into a shallow, hastily shoveled trench alongside the fence that bordered the potato field, and the barnyard further down.

Eventually—for the mud continued to be a problem —the new spring was provided with a neat stone-lined basin, and the pipes that had carried water down from the old springhouse to the barn were dug up and relaid from the new one. "I know it's not for long," Granny had fussed, "but I cannot abide a job half done."

From spring planting time onward, farm workdays always stretched from dawn to dusk. Now, with Trashbin laid up, Petey and his grandmother often were out for three or four hours after supper, finishing up by lantern light or in the bleached-blue shadows of an early-rising moon. The chickens, because of the danger from varmints, were moved, with their perches and straw-filled orange-crate nests, to the barn. The overflow of Trashbin's bottle collection was shifted out of the two end stalls and up to the chicken coop to make room for them.

It was Petey's idea that the bottles, strung up by

their necks on cords or wires to clank and twinkle above the vegetable garden, might keep the birds away. Tied in clusters in the tops of apple trees and festooned from oak to maple to oak along the outer fencerows, they proved quite useful. A wandering groundhog, who one night discovered the cornfield below the orchard and stripped half of it down to mere nubbins of stalks before Granny stung him in the nose with a load of buckshot, tripped the new bottle burglar alarm the next night and fled in confusion.

Happily, there were bottles aplenty. Boxes more from the barn loft and stacks of old magazines were shifted to the chicken coop, along with bundles of wire coat hangers, gunnysacks full of flannel strips scavenged from the trash barrels of the Mosstown Pajama Manufactory, and assorted items of ironmongery from the county dump. Trashbin might turn his face to the bedroom wall when asked to lend a hand at this or that, but Granny had to admit that without his bottles the farm might well have been plucked clean.

But if it was not plucked clean, when the late summer rains came it was in grave danger of being washed entirely away. Thundershowers, which in Mosstown gently cleared the air and freshened leaves and flowers, battered unmercifully at the little farm on the ridge. Every drop was a heavy splash. In the fields, water gurgled down the rows. In the vegetable garden rivulets met and spread downhill in a muddy sheet. Plants heavy with tomatoes sagged away from their stakes, and onions heeled over in droves. Only the straw hastily strewn up one soggy row and down the next kept the vegetables from being washed loose.

This near-disaster was a clear warning that much more mulch would be needed in the months before winter: straw, hay, grass cuttings, leaves, anything to protect the precious topsoil—even weeds. Granny gritted her teeth and gave up pulling weeds until they were half-grown, and then they went on the compost heap with the kitchen garbage to rot into fertilizer-mulch. "Waste not, want not," said Granny grimly.

Once or twice, sitting in the kitchen whittling while Granny shelled peas and the rain drummed loudly on the roof, Petey thought uneasily, "The Professor might be at Lake Meander by now," or, "Maybe he's in Poconomee now." But he didn't say it aloud.

It was not until September that Granny, alarmed by the first falling leaves, packed up a lunch and supper so that Petey could have another try at reaching help. Equipped with a coil of rope and a vague notion of how to build a raft, he came safely to the creek at the edge of the old Sampson place.

White Oak Creek was in full spate after the recent rains. It frothed and roiled like an angry river among the rocks and was within inches of overflowing its banks. Petey's first attempt at lashing several log-sized twigs together to make a narrow raft came apart in the rushing current. Fortunately, one end of the rope had been snubbed around a nearby laurel bush.

The second attempt, two logs wider and well-braced by being lashed to two stout crosspieces, was more successful as a raft, but it was not to be a happy success. Once in the water it and the tied-down picnic basket bobbed and dipped encouragingly—until Petey loosened the rope and prepared to leap aboard. Then it bucked like a Wild West bronco, swirled away from the bank, and swooped downstream, trailing the rope behind.

The loss of the rope and the picnic basket was discouraging, but worse was the realization that it might be summertime again before the creek was calm and shallow enough to pole a raft along. The farm had survived so far, but winter was quite another thing. A little frightened, and trying not to think of the shipwrecked (by now) lunch, Petey scuffed his way along the bank. Of course, he *could* go the long way, by the road, sleeping out and eating berries, but sleeping out, with its danger from night-hunting creatures, was even more dangerous than braving the dogs who lived along the Mosstown road.

By an ugly streamside dump he had seen-but-not-seen dozens of times before, Petey dawdled to a stop. Could he get to town in a rusty sardine can? There was a wooden picnic spoon that might do for a paddle. But the tin, once in the water, promptly swamped itself and sank. Discouraged, Petey poked through the trash, thinking there might at least be something useful to take home to Granny.

There wasn't. But on an impulse he upended a squat wide-mouthed medicine bottle and unscrewed the cap. Taking the letters to the Judge and the Reverend and Miss Ample, he stuffed them inside and replaced the top. One good shove rolled the bottle down the bank. It bobbed and dipped and swept downstream out of sight. Petey shivered. It was better than nothing. They had managed so far without help. They could keep on a bit longer.

After an early cold snap, complete with a powdering of snow, on Halloween, winter changed its mind and held off until the week before Christmas. There was time to stack the outside walls of both barn and house high with firewood. Most of this was brought by wagon from the great woods across the wasteland northwest of the orchard. The ground there was littered with fat dry twigs and branches whipped off by the wind. To everyone's surprise, the cow Daisy had agreed to work in harness with Jenny, and once a roadway of sorts had been cleared among the stones, the firewood piled up as rapidly as Petey could drive the wagon and load it up.

Stacking the wood was important too, for the cordwood made a sort of overcoat for house and barn. Granny fretted about the danger of wood lice and termites, but there was at least no danger from them down at the barn, where the walls of the ground floor were mortared stone.

Between alarms over varmints and invasions of insects, Petey drove back and forth with Jenny and Daisy. Granny saw to the winter's stores. She had a new root cellar, and there, in boxes lined with fresh straw, she stored carrots and onions, potatoes, turnips, and rutabagas. There was a barrel of McIntosh apples and one of Winesaps, and a third and fourth of the pippins that had made her apple spice cake and deep-dish apple pies famous at church picnics.

Evenings were spent adding to the rows of mason jars that lined the kitchen and hall cupboards. There were vegetables in jars, plain, preserved, and pickled, peaches glowing in apple brandy, honey, candied cherries, jars of jellies, jams and preserves gleaming like jewels in the corner cupboard, from pale translucent gooseberries and ruby raspberries to the rich dark glint of blackberries. Good things ripened in earthen jugs (and the glass jugs from Trashbin's collection that were too heavy to hang in the treetops): cider and apple brandy, root beer and elderberry wine.

In the barn every corner and cranny was put to use. In the loft, hay was piled to the rafters. The grain bin, as well as the outdoor corncrib—which had been re-assembled without its roof in one corner of the loft—bulged with what corn the groundhog had left, but mostly with large acorns. Granny, worried by the barley and oats lost to a passing family of field mice, had opined that if pigs liked acorns, why shouldn't cows? But the two bushels she gathered under the oaks below the barn and along the fencerows had barely covered the bottom of the grain bin.

"A sight puny this year, ain't they?" A smile had creased her little dried-apple face. " 'Course we're all a sight puny, but I mean besides that."

"Mebbe they lost some roots, them big oaks," guessed Petey. "Being just at the edges all 'round the farm like they are."

Granny, still thinking her own thoughts, did not hear. "But not *all* acorns are puny, now, are they? Only the ones here on the farm." Her eyes, black as currants, gleamed.

"You could crack a big one with a sledgehammer," Petey offered.

Granny nodded. "And scrape out the meal and mash it up with a bit of grain and hot water. Make a nice feed cake, it should."

"No harm trying."

That afternoon Petey fetched the first wagonload of acorns from across the waste, and Granny was proved right, as usual.

"No harm trying" sounds a matter-of-fact way of going about things, but in a quiet fashion it is really quite adventuresome. Petey and Granny found that even ideas that began as jokes could turn out to be very practical indeed.

Deep cold and deep snow were as dangerous as they were inconvenient. A modest three-inch fall was waist-high, and the three-foot drifts of deep winter could smother the farm completely. Even though the winds blowing down across the waste scoured through the trees and down across the fields and gardens, the first snow drifted almost to the eaves of the farmhouse on the leeward back-porch side. Digging a path to the barn the long way around, from the front door, took from daybreak until midmorning.

"The snow fences wouldn't've done a lick of good even if I'd got them up," Petey complained at lunch-time, warming his face in the steam from a bowl of chicken soup with homemade egg noodles. "Snow's too deep, and the fence's too short. One strung up flat-ways in the air'd keep a sight more snow off."

"Well, then? No harm trying just that." Granny put down the bread knife and set a third slice across two edgeways ones, like a roof. "Now, if you could make the top *slanty*, so's the snow wouldn't weigh so heavy on it. . . ."

At dinnertime Petey remarked that already the ma-nure pile was bare of snow. "Steamin' away like a fur-

nace. I s'pose I got to shift it, so's it don't heat up the woodpile and burn up the whole shebang.''

Granny nodded thoughtfully as she ladled chicken gravy over his mound of mashed potatoes. "Now there's another thought worth trying," she said after a minute.

She chuckled and explained.

Two days later, when the snow had melted, Petey dug the postholes that would extend the long rose arbor the last twenty feet up to the back porch and another twenty at the bottom end down to the new spring—the stretch where the drifting had been worst. With the posts set, the upper framework was nailed together. Then, taking care not to damage the leafless tangle of rambler roses, he and Granny unrolled the rolls of snow fence and tied them, two high, along each side of the tunnel arbor. Two more, wired together, made a long, peaked, slat roof.

The next morning Petey and the wheelbarrow plied between the manure pile and the new spring, along the line of the new water pipe. Before lunch a neat rounded hummock of a path, tidily covered with straw, reached from the downhill side of the spring right to the barn door. The heat from the rotting manure would not only afford a snow-free path, but it meant the end of frozen pipes and the numberless buckets of water carried to the barn in other winters.

But "no harm trying" had its own dangers. Though the MacCubbins talked among themselves of "When Constable Dudley catches up with old Lilliput-Kurtz . . ." or "When we *do* get to town and all's right again, mind I don't forget that quilt I promised for the missionary barrel," and such things, there began to be more enjoyment in plotting answers to the problems spring would bring.

"The 'taties and carrots did fair, but the turnip and beetroot greens got chewed to rags. Why'n't the creatures go for your old garlic and red peppers and such too?" "Um. They don't like mint either. What about a nice smelly salad dressing spray for the greens: garlic and pepper and mint?

"Come spring, there's no straw for mulch, Gran'. We'll get washed down to Mosstown." "Now there's a thought. Moss. There's moss grows thick as a rug up above the old woodlot. If you could get the wagon up there, I 'spect you could just slice it up and roll it in nice green bales. No harm trying."

And so it went.

But there is no makeshift for a doctor. Trashbin's cough grew more and more hollow, and his cheeks too. He was moved to a bed set up by the parlor fireplace, and Granny dosed him with dock weed syrup and pennyroyal tea and hot footbaths, but they did no good. Horseradish plasters, mullein tea, nothing helped.

As Trashbin pined away, he grew gentle and almost considerate. For Christmas he gave Granny a jug stopper he had whittled in the shape of a small, smiling, bonneted Granny. To Petey he gave—at last—the fatal Hudson roadster, tied up in brown paper with a fancy-knotted string. He died just at the end of the January thaw, a thaw so warm that the lilac buds had come by mistake. They were nipped in the bud together.

Eight

WHEN WINTER COMES, SPRING ISN'T FAR BEHIND. OR
summer or autumn. Even with sixteen-hour workdays, there was scarcely time to catch a breath between
chores. Plowing, sowing, and cultivating, dawn-to-
dusk jobs in themselves, were complicated at Lost
Farm (as Petey had dubbed it) by the insects, some
nasty, all greedy, and a few downright vicious. They
kept at it from last thaw to first freeze. Only the full-
size ladybugs, three MacCubbin inches long and
vaguely friendly—except to aphids—were any sort of
help. Against the varmints—mice, squirrels, chip-
munks, weasels and foxes—the only defenses were
barred doors. When, after a time, stringy grass grew
up in the wasteland, deer came there at dusk to bed
down, and the hunting varmints kept away. There
were some thirty deer in the herd, but they never
strayed through the thicket of shrunken oaks and maples. Large as they were, and silent as ghosts moving

out in the gray dawn, they were still a lovely welcome sight to Pete and Granny.

That year—it was 1923—the only chance Petey had to try again for town was on a dismal rainy day when the downpour was too heavy for him to do any field work. The attempt came to a soggy end when Jenny, whose memory was long, refused to set a foot off the farm. Head down, ears back, she stood like a stone in the rain on the "safe" side of the boundary and budged only when a soaked and sneezing Petey pulled her head back toward the barn.

Eventually the flour barrel was emptied, and the raided cornfield never yielded much more than the next year's seed corn. The beets and spinach damped off, and the second winter the lopsided cherry tree toppled under a weight of snow. But for every loss there was a find. Acorn meat not only made a superior cattle mash, but dried and pounded proved an excellent flour. For greens, there were chickweed, jewelweed, and goose grass. Red haws and wild rose hips were, to Petey's mind, better than cherries any day.

To Petey's way of thinking, today was better than yesterday, too. Every today was better than any yesterday simply because it was . . . more real. The outside world slipped further and further away despite Granny's still saying half a dozen times a day that she meant to do this or that "soon as you get to town and we get set right." Evenings, by the kitchen fire, she told exciting tales of the Civil War or read to Petey from old *Saturday Evening Post*s. She did all the voices in the stories and sang ballads in a quavery soprano to the sad-sweet notes of her old dulcimer and so kept bits and pieces of the Outside alive.

Petey entertained Granny in turn by spinning preposterous plans for covering the good-as-fifty miles to Mosstown. Pointing one evening to an illustration of an elephant with a howdah on its back in one of the *Post* stories, he allowed as he could weave a contraption something like that with willow withies.

"You could ride down in style in the basket like this here Indian princess in her thingumajig, Granny, and I'd sit forward and steer, like the fellow in the turban."

"Just what sort of beast do you aim to ride us down on?" Granny asked drily. "Groundhogs, now, they may be friendlier than most, but they've a terrible lolloping gallop. Passengers that wasn't flung out would surely perish from discombobulation."

"I thought of that," said Petey soberly. "I thought we'd snare us a bird and gentle it. A good-sized robin, mebbe, or a purple martin."

Granny's eyes twinkled as she shook her head emphatically. "Not a martin, thank you," she said. "Too swoopy by a long sight, like all their swallow cousins. I'm not a one for roller coasters."

If swoopers and darters were out, what was needed, Petey declared, was a biggish glider sort of bird. The farm's weather, because of the shape of the hills just there, usually came down from the northwest, and a good breeze should soar them right down to town. They agreed to "think on it."

Several days of half-serious, half-funning bird-watching narrowed the local field down to a pair of chicken hawks that circled over the farm from time to time. The very thought gave Granny the shivers. "A mouse would be safer trying to catch a ride on a cat!"

Another time, prompted by an old magazine article about "The Secret of the Pyramids," Petey proposed jacking up the house and, using great logs as rollers, proceeding down to town in comfortable stages. Jenny and the cattle and pigs, sheep, and dogs—by day harnessed up in long lines like the toiling Egyptian slaves pulling their massive blocks of stone—would, at each nightly halt, for safety's sake be brought up a ramp and stabled in the parlor and two spare bedrooms with the chickens and cats. "No, it won't do," was Granny's prim answer. "I pos-i-tively draw the line at chickens roosting on the stair rail and bulls in the same parlor with my chiney cupboard."

Granny did not always see the jokes coming. One evening after putting a pan of black-eyed peas to soak for the morrow, and giving a second honey-sweetening to the half-brewed barrel of ale in the cupboard next to the stove, she found Petey at the parlor table, laboriously lettering on a large scrap of torn sheet: HELP! BRING SHERIFF TO MACCUBBINS'. Her entire dustrag collection of worn-out sheets was stacked at his elbow.

"Huntin' season isn't far off," he said solemnly. "I figured if I tied a message to the antlers of every buck deer out in the grasslands before they move on up the ridge, word'd be bound to get through. Them hunters get a buck or two out of this bunch every year."

"*Those* hunters," gasped Granny before collapsing in a flutter onto the good horsehair upholstered settee. It was too dangerous. He would be trampled. Bucks were so much more wary than does. One whiff of human and. . . .

Petey, about to burst with laughter, gave in. "Gosh,

Granny, even if I got close enough, and they was curled up fast asleep with their chins on the ground, deer hair's so stiff and slickery I'd never make it up unless I took a stepladder to get atop their noses. I was just funnin'."

But beneath the fun lay worry. Granny fretted herself with thinking, "What if help never came?" One day Petey would be left by his lonesome. What then? It was this thought that set Granny to begin her *Book of Hereabouts Yarbs* (as she called herbs) *and Usefull Knowlidge* in an old school exercise book. In it she noted down her recipes, both the old favorites for which ingredients could still be come by, and such additions as rose-hip cordial, birch-flour bread, acorn-and-currant pudding, and red haw and beechnut pies. There were practical directions for making vinegar from apple parings, for making yeast, for tanning leather, sewing moccasins, mittens and boots, and making turpentine and soap and candles. Here and there warnings popped up, such as *ALWAYS clean the Stove 1st thing in the Morning & save Ashes for the garden or Soap*, and *BEWARE eating Rabbitts large or small after Midsummer for fear of the Warbles*, or

When caught by a Tempest, wherever you be,
If it lightens and thunders, beware of a Tree.

For ailments, there were remedies: wild mint tea for a fever, wintergreen tea for a touch of the "Rheumaticks," chickweed poultices for boils, and marsh-marigold juice for warts. Insects, she noted, disliked pennyroyal; and a good rub of squashed jewelweed was best against poison ivy. Against garden pests, childhood lore and keen observation had taught Granny more tricks than her pepper and garlic spray. She knew that horseradish in the potato patch discouraged potato beetles; that snails and slugs would happily drown themselves in saucers of home-brewed beer; that basil growing among the tomatoes helped ward off tomato worms; and much more.

When eventually the exercise book was filled, margins and all, Granny carefully abstracted the blank endpapers from the books on the parlor shelves—the sets of Richardson's and Miss Austen's novels and Dr. Johnson's *Lives of the Poets* she had brought to the ridge as a bride. Sewn into booklets, these too were soon covered with neat tiny script. When the last snippets of paper ran out, Granny set to making her own. With care, pages could be peeled from a square of birch bark like sheets from a tablet.

As the years passed and Granny grew more frail, and more reconciled to their little world in the great woods, she tucked thoughtful little sayings in between the recipes. There was *Every Path hath its Puddle,* and

> *Hard Times and Backaches are pretty much alike—*
> *An ounce of Liniment is worth a heap of Lamen-*
> *tation.*

and

> *If you would enjoy the Fruit, pluck not the Flower.*

From the little table by the parlor window Granny was watching and listening to Petey, at work down in the barnyard, singing at the top of his lungs. After a moment she put down her quill pen and smiled at what she had written:

> *He that follows Nature is never out of his Way.*

She drew a small sigh. "Even if he's been put out of ever'body else's way."

In the barnyard Petey was singing "Green Grow the Rushes, Ho!", a cheerful sound that brushed away all shadows. "No sense borrowing trouble," thought Granny, straightening resolutely. "That way you have to pay for it twice."

Then she wrote that down too.

Nine

PETEY WAS SHOOTING UP LIKE A WEED. "A HANDSOME boy," Granny thought proudly; and all too soon it was, "A fine young man." More and more he reminded her of her own dear Malcolm, lost on a long-ago battlefield. "A fine young man," she whispered, bestowing one of her warm papery kisses on the old daguerreotype portrait of a mustachioed young man in a Union uniform.

From Petey's fifteenth birthday, when she had to fetch the stepping stool before she could reach high enough to mark his year's growth—a hand's breadth—on the kitchen doorpost, Granny took to calling him "Pete" instead of "Petey." "Because that 'y' means "little!" She laughed. "A 'diminutive,' it's called; and whatever you are, my dear, you're not diminutive anymore."

"But you are." Pete grinned. "So I reckon I'd better stick to 'Granny' and leave off 'Gran.' " If anything, with age and the twinges of arthritis, Granny grew smaller with the years.

The continual struggle to keep the farm alive did not diminish. Still, in his rare and too-short breathing spells, Pete tried plan after plan for reaching town. Walking was altogether out now, even though he had grown strong and wary enough to brave its risks. Granny could no longer be left alone for so long to cope with chores and varmints. Jenny never could be persuaded off the property, but after she died at twenty-two (a ripe old age for a mule), Pete hit upon the idea of training one of the young steers to saddle —they could run at a fast enough clip when they'd a mind to. That project fizzled out after a wasted summer. Wynken, a sheep-witted creature, spooked too easily and was next to impossible to guide with the reins. Blynken was no better, and Nod, after his first lesson, turned crazy-mean at the sight of a bridle.

"Why they call 'em steers when you can't steer 'em worth a hill of beans, *I'll* never know," complained Pete on the evening he gave it up. "It's time that Nod was turned into steaks and beef bacon."

Some years slipped by so filled with work and worries that only Granny's hand-drawn kitchen calendars proved that they were past. Dates meant little. It was the excitement of some danger or adventure or some fresh plan for getting down to Mosstown that set one year apart from another. The winter of 1930, for instance, was the Automatic Wagon Winter. The wide aisle between the barn stalls was littered with old iron for the new project. Night after night Pete fired up a small makeshift forge and hammered away at angle-irons, braces, a flywheel arm, and iron sheathing to reinforce the new oaken axle with a U-bend in the middle that he had shaped for the wagon. Brooding over the little Hudson car one evening, he had suddenly taken it into his head that the old five-horsepower motor buried somewhere among Trashbin's junk in the old chicken coop might be worth having a look at. It was seized up with rust and had to be soaked in the last of the hoarded kerosene, then taken apart and painstakingly cleaned, but the day it coughed into life and ran for ten minutes on a cupful of potato alcohol, Pete felt he was halfway to a motor wagon. He said nothing to Granny, for fear of getting her hopes up, and though Granny asked no questions about all the whanging and clanging, she did a lot of guessing.

By the spring day when he was at last ready for a test run, Pete could no longer hide his excitement.

"Granny! Where've you got to?" He rushed through the kitchen and hallway and called up the stairs. "Granny!"

"Whatever is it?" Granny, a trifle dazed, opened the door to the cupboard under the stairs, which he had slammed in passing, and peered out. "I might've dropped the pickle crock," she chided.

"Pickles! Who cares about pickles?" Laughing, Pete hustled her ahead of him to the back door. "I got something to show you down to the barn."

"Now, this here big wheel," he was soon explaining, "used to drive a belt that moved another wheel on, say, a pump. But it ain't strong enough to turn a wagon axle that way, so I bolted on this arm here—" He pointed to an iron bar, flattened at the bolted end, which extended from the motor flywheel down through

(79)

a hole in the wagon bed and at its bottom was bent around the front axle at the middle of the U-bend. "Now looky here." He gave the starter three swift turns.

"Land sakes!" Granny gasped as the engine caught. The wheel turned slowly, and the rod dipped down and up. The U-bend in the new light axle was pushed around in a slow flip-flop. The wagon creaked forward as its wheels completed a full turn.

"Land sakes *alive!*" said Granny. "If that doesn't beat all!"

Red-faced with pride and excitement, Pete lifted her onto the high front wagon seat and climbed up beside her. The motor, just below and behind, had to be started up again and Pete, reaching over the back of the seat, opened the throttle a shade wider this time. "The steering's sort of make-do still," he said modestly, "and I got to mend the brake shoes, but she'll do for here on the flat." He took up two ropes attached like reins to the light frame replacing the old wagon tongue. Pulling on the right-hand rope, he managed a neat—if creaky—turn into the stretch of road below the barn.

"I got to grease the axle fittings, too," Pete yelled as he opened up the throttle on the motor as far as it would go. There was a good hundred yards of straight-away before the Waste. "Hang on, Granny. We're off!"

"We may be off," Granny said tartly two minutes later, "but we ain't running. I could do a sight better on foot."

Pete was crestfallen. They were putt-putting along

at a snail's pace. "I don't understand it. I clocked them front wheels at near a hundred turns a minute. 'Course, the whole rig was still jacked up off the ground. That might make a difference, I suppose. I reckoned the wagon ought to do five miles an hour, same as I can afoot, but it could keep going dawn-to-dusk and not get tired. So long as you had good brakes, you wouldn't even need the motor on the downhill bits."

An acrid smell of hot oil and hotter metal rose from the straining motor. "Mebbe one of those old brake shoes has jammed fast. I'll just have a look."

Pete slid to the end of the seat and leaped down into the road, thinking to walk alongside until he figured out what was wrong. But no sooner was he clear, than the wagon took off with a clatter and a shriek. The shriek was Granny's. The clatter was the motor, which without Pete's weight (for he was a tall young man) did not have to strain so.

Granny—who had not gone so fast since her last ride in a proper horse-drawn buggy—swore afterward that with her bonnet strings a-flap and Pete standing amazed in the road behind, she thought her time had come. "I'd had a good eighty-two years," she said, "and I'm not a one to quibble with the good Lord when he says, 'Time's up,' but I did think it a pity just then with me all flustered and unprepared. *And* in my garden shoes and second-best bonnet."

The wagon rolled steadily on, and only when Pete came trotting up to the tailgate did the old lady realize how little danger there was. Hopping aboard, Pete throttled down the engine, set the brakes, and then lifted Granny from her perch.

Then it happened. The worn brake shoe fell off, and the wheels, freed, began to turn. Either vibration or some defect in the throttle urged the motor from clack to whirr to hum and sent the empty wagon down the road at a surprising clip. Had the stretch of road been longer, Pete could have caught up at a trot, but the wagon dipped down onto the Deer Field, as they now called the Waste, and fetched up in the towering grass against a great rock.

With a broken front axle.

"I'll put the old one back on it." Pete, inspecting the damage, was philosophical. "Reckon I didn't allow near enough for the weight of the wagon, and I plumb forgot to figure in the passengers and load. Knuckle-head MacCubbin and his Mile-an-Hour Motor Wagon!" He drew a deep breath and managed a grin. "Leastways the motor's not hurt. Mebbe I'll just hitch it up to that little old hand mill of yours. How does 'The MacCubbin Power Flour Grinder' sound?"

"It sounds right nice." Granny, still a bit fluttered, tied her sunbonnet strings in a straggly bow. "My old elbows aren't what they used to be when I could grind all morning and then whip up an angel food cake to pop in the oven before lunch. As for getting to town," she added firmly, "don't you fret. Where there's a will, there's a way."

Will or no, the way was tiresomely elusive. The year Granny was eighty-four, Pete finally launched a good solid raft on White Oak Creek and poled it downstream three hundred yards—only to be brought up short by a recently built beaver dam. Several young

buck beavers thought it great fun swamping the little raft with ripples from the slap of their tails.

On Granny's eighty-ninth—on the very day itself—an airplane circled above the farm. It was the first they had ever seen outside the pages of the *Post*. An excited Pete snatched up his tinderbox and ran for the grassy Deer Field. The aviator in the little double-winged plane buzzing along beneath the thick gray clouds certainly saw the signal blaze Pete set in a patch of tall grass standing by itself among the rocks, but it all came to nothing. The little plane did circle back several times like a persistent dragonfly, drawn by the bright flames when the wind whipped the sparks of Pete's small blaze into the grass beyond the rocks, but when lightning flickered and the rain finally broke, it skittered off.

At first there seemed no real damage done. The cloudburst had drenched the flames before any trees were more than singed. But with the grass gone, much of the scanty topsoil was washed away in the afternoon-long deluge. The Deer Field was once again "The Waste." The following spring saw a patchy growth, but not enough for the deer, who found softer beds in the bracken hollows higher on the ridge. Several families of field mice and diehard moles remained, and the varmints came hunting them. A bobcat came down once before the last snow had melted, and the mild April evenings brought, in alarming succession, a skunk, a tall gray fox, a wild tabby cat and, worst of all, a weasel. The weasel got the steer Pete had just harnessed to the plow in the south field and might as easily have got Pete instead if he had looked as tasty as the steer. And so it went. After six weeks of spraying pepper mixture around the boundaries in hopes of turning away these curious sniffing interlopers and continually refurbishing the alarm-and-trap festoons of bottles, Pete counted up the losses, surveyed the broken glass and the growing backlog of essential work, and came to a grim conclusion.

"I don't see as we have much choice, Granny," he announced one suppertime in early June. "It's 'Get up and get out' or face worse times than we've had yet. It's all my fault—settin' that dang-fool fire—and there's no sense your sufferin' for it. I figure we could make the trip in easy stages. Camp out on the way. One of the cows could pull a sort of Indian *travois* with wheels on it, if I was to lead her. We'd take a cookpot and food enough, and with a featherbed on top, you could ride in style. We'd take Mutt and young Florence. They're the best watchdogs we got." He thoughtfully fingered the moustache he had started in honor of his twenty-eighth birthday and avoided Granny's dumbfounded stare. "We'd need an ax—for firewood and raft logs— and you could braid all that linen you spun from last year's flax into good fine rope, to be sure we had enough. I'll have to build a second raft below that beaver pond." He busied himself with his fork and a large slice of apple crumb pie.

Granny was stunned. The boy was serious! He sat there, looking the spit and image of his grandfather, her dear Malcolm, and talked of abandoning the farm.

"I've never been 'shamed of you, Peter MacCubbin," she quavered, "and I don't rightly know how to begin now, but—such talk! I'm puckered just to hear

(85)

it. As if I'm not up to a bit of hardship and a good lot of work still," she finished indignantly.

Pete downed his fork and faced her, a little flushed, and pleadingly, but with a stubborn set to his jaw. For the first time Granny saw in him a touch of his great-granddaddy, old Horsefeathers.

"There's no two ways about it," said Pete. "Down to town is more'n a two-day trip afoot *or* on the water. It takes time to build a raft. And even then it'd be a while before the law could track down the Professor and his infernal machine." He held up a hand to stop her protest. "I know you got spunk enough to face six varmints 'twixt lunch and supper, but hauling feed and shoveling muck is heavy work, and you're lighter'n a dried-up apple blossom. Why, one weasel sneeze'd blow you clean away."

"Hmph!" Granny snorted. "I've sense enough to keep indoors when *they're* about."

"But if one of 'em took to hanging around," Pete went on doggedly, "you couldn't get down to feed the stock at all. And what if you was caught out in the open? I know you ain't using a cane just yet, but I don't see you dashing around like you used to, neither. The old place'll still be here when we get back. We're losing stock as it is. Most likely lose a lot more, go or stay."

It made sense. Granny saw that. But all the while she was allowing herself to be persuaded, a cold lump of misery rose beneath her breastbone. She thrust it down and was careful to seem cheerful for Pete's sake. "Imagine *me* a Fearful Flora," she scolded herself. "It's about *time* I got out and about."

(86)

Two days later they set out. Pete's travois was easily put together: two long poles fastened at one end to a harness, braced in the middle, and at the back end provided with a series of braces making a stout platform. Wheeled, and loaded with parcels of provisions tied down under a wrapping of blankets, it made quite a comfortable seat. The only disadvantage was that, as Granny discovered, riding backward she had to watch the farm until the road took up beyond the Waste and it dwindled out of sight:

It was more than she could bear.

Pete, coming back when next he stopped Milly the cow for a rest, found the old lady in tears.

"I can't b-bear it," Granny sobbed. "I'll never see the dear place again. I *know* I shan't. My rosebushes and the lilac trees . . . and the dear bridal spruces my Malcolm planted out front that first day here after we were wed." Tears ran down the wrinkles in her pink cheeks faster than she could brush them away. "I-I'll be all right by and by," she wavered.

Pete leaned down to give her a kiss and then went to turn Milly back toward the farm.

Ten

A LOT OF WATER FLOWED DOWN OLD WAY CREEK AND
into White Oak Creek between the day Pete turned
Milly around and the day he went out to gather late
May apples in the big woods and, what with one thing
and another, nearly ended in being gathered himself.
Granny had died years before, at the marvelous age of
one hundred five, but Pete had never made the
long trip in to Mosstown because by then the Warneckis had moved into the old Sampson place. Having
the Warneckis spread across your path was pretty much
like having a hornet's nest hanging just outside your
door.

The Warneckis—Mr. and Mrs. and five sharp-faced,
runny-nosed children, seven skinny-ribbed hound dogs,
and an ancient Ford truck piled high with rabbit
hutches and topped off with a birdcage crammed full
of frantic bantam chickens—had looked at first like an
answer to prayer. If Pete had not grown wary as a wild

animal in his years up on the ridge, he might have had a very nasty surprise.

Instead, by turns fascinated and mistrustful, he had watched them, now and again taking a day off from field work, packing a lunch and supper, and making for the tangled strip of trees and brush and wild grape-vines between White Oak Creek and the road past Warneckis' front yard. Safe in a high perch gained with the help of the vines and long thorns that could be climbed like ladder rungs, Pete watched and listened. The dogs paced and whined in a too-small pen. The children tormented the wretched bantam cock and chased the poor witless hens until they looked like be-draggled feather dusters. Mrs. Warnecki nagged hope-lessly. But it was seeing Mr. Warnecki setting bird snares and spring traps in the woods and nailing var-mint hides to dry on the barn door that decided Pete against approaching such folk for help. Anyone who'd snare meadowlarks. . . .

Still, he could have got past the Warneckis, and would have, had it not been for the raccoon. Some Sat-urday nights Mr. Warnecki and a friend or three took dogs and guns and jugs up the ridge—always, Pete was thankful, in the opposite direction from Old Way Creek—whooping and hollering half the night long after raccoons. Sunday mornings usually saw another hide on the barn door.

One Sunday there was a live raccoon in a hutch in the front yard instead. An old gray-muzzled fellow, he had probably been dragged down from the lower branches of a tree he was too winded to climb. It wrung Pete's heart to see him hunkered down in a corner of the wire box, dipping dry bread crusts and apple parings in a pan of filthy water (for the children never changed it), and now and again slowly running a thin black finger down the wire mesh wall. Pete gathered from the children's remarks that they were keeping him for their eldest brother, Hank, who traveled with a two-bit carnival as keeper of a menagerie. "Worth four, five dollars, that animal," Mr. Warnecki had said, sounding like a harsher version of Trashbin.

The lock to the cage was only a rusty hasp fastened by a wooden pin. Temptation became determination. One evening just at dusk, when the Warneckis were at their supper, Pete slipped across the dusty road, under the listing gate, and climbed up the coarse screen. But the pin was jammed more tightly than he had expected, and no amount of pushing would dislodge it. Reluctantly abandoning the attempt, Pete was on his way down again when he caught sight of the smallest and nastiest Warnecki emerging openmouthed from the shrubbery by the front steps. There was a gasp, a slapping of bare feet across the porch floor, and the crash of the slammed screen door. The yell that accompanied the slam sent Pete tearing pell-mell back across the road.

"*Paw*! Paw, come *quick*! There's a-a little chipmunk man a-tryin' to set that old coon loose. *PAW*? *He's* mine if you ketch him. I seed him first. You *hear*? I betcha Hank'll give me a *hunderd* dollars fer a little chipmunk man!"

From the safety of his perch Pete saw the canny old raccoon reach up, wriggle the peg loose, then replace it and return to his corner as the yard was flooded with dogs and children. He would bide his time.

Pete's own escape, along a stout branch overhanging the creek and down a wild grapevine, took him home by a roundabout route. He crossed the creek twice again, higher up, by the same trick, to be sure of losing the dogs.

But that was years ago. The Warneckis, who had kept such a sharp eye out for the "little chipmunk man," were gone now. Had *been* gone for over a year. And here he still was. Life on the farm was good now, if not always comfortable, and after the Warneckis, Pete had begun to wonder if the outside world was worth reaching. There were new people in the old Sampson place, but he kept putting off "going down to have a look-see." Next week would do. And the next week had always provided more work and more excuses. Today, however, there was not an excuse in sight. There was, to judge from the sound, a largish group of people moving through the woods higher up. Pete, torn by caution and curiosity, took off after them.

"They surely do make a racket," Pete muttered to his old dog Belle. "I never heard such a ruckus since Tabby got in amongst the hens. Cackle, cackle, cackle!"

Pete's patience was wearing thin. He had tracked the party of hikers for what seemed miles, and though he could hear laughter and voices, they were still well ahead. The gully here was like a channel down the mountainside, and sound flowed down it.

"I'll be blowed. Sounds like children laughin'!" Pete stopped to listen, a slow smile spreading above his gingery beard. He leaned down to scratch Belle under the chin. "Never heard such a thing before, did you, old girl? Well, now ain't the time to get acquainted. You stay to heel and keep quiet, and we'll see if we can catch 'em up."

There had been no one but hunters in these high woods for years, and lately not many of those except for a few old-timers in deer season. The road up above the old Sampson place had washed out years ago, and travelers afoot usually followed the south fork of White Oak Creek up to the ridge. The brush had grown up so that you couldn't tell Old Way Creek was there at all. It slid into the north branch of the White Oak from under a ledge of overhanging rock, and green-briar and wild grapevines curtained the old road from even the sharpest eyes.

"They could've got hold of an old map," Pete thought. "A danged nuisance, that's what it is, folks traipsing through in summertime." Summertime was for tending crops and sitting in the cool green shade, not for keeping a watch out for trespassers. "Danged nuisance."

Far up the hill a "Halloo!" rang out. A man's voice.

"Halloo the end of the line! We've come the wrong way after all. The creek peters out. But it's not far to the top. Hurry up, and we'll take fifteen minutes for lunch before we come down again." There was a pause, then an anxious "Halloo the end of the line! You there?"

The answering call came from so close by that Pete and old Belle froze in alarm.

"Halloo above! You lead on without us, Macduff.

(92)

You can collect us on the way back down."

There was a disapproving silence from the head of the line and then, nearby, a second speaker, a woman, chuckled. "Poor Brother Ed. I can hear him now, apologizing for his eccentric sister. But we'll just let him cluck. There's too much to see to go charging uphill like twenty Teddy Roosevelts. I half thought I saw a hermit thrush light down in that sumac over there. Who's got my bird glasses?"

Pete had almost run smack into the hikers' rear guard, and to make things even more alarming, there was something about that voice . . . an echo of long ago. But then, it was a fair time since he had heard any voice at all. Before he quite realized it, he had dropped the lunch basket and sack of May apples, propped his shotgun against a young tree, signed "Stay" to Belle, and headed up the slope. Coming to the clearing where the hikers had halted, he took shelter behind an ancient beech. His heart pounded. For years he had taken to his heels at the first sign of another human being. "Most dangerous animals in the woods," Granny had always said. Hunters were crazy enough—some of them would shoot anything that moved—but Them Others (by which Granny meant the rest of the world), "they see some purty little thing, or one a bit out of the way of your ordinary run o' things, and they'll pull it up by the roots to see how it grows or chop it down and tote it home. Paint it purple and put it in a pickle jar, most like. No sense atall, most of 'em."

That was what made them dangerous. But even as Pete reminded himself of just that, he was sidling

around the great tree trunk until, screened by the shiny
dark leaves of a mountain laurel, he could see and hear
without being seen.

The one the children called Miss Bostweiler sat on a
rock and surveyed the staghorn sumac tree through a
small pair of field glasses. She was not unlike a small
brown bird herself: middling tall, but very thin and
very quick, as if her skinny bones were hollow, like a
wren's. She wore a pair of faded khaki shorts, a Snoopy
T-shirt, and tennis shoes. Her berry-brown arms and
legs were crisscrossed with bramble scratches old and
new, and her short salt-and-pepper gray hair stuck up
on top where the cord on the field glasses had ruffled
it. "There's a white-breasted nuthatch," she announced, putting down the glasses, "but no hermit
thrush. We've scared him away. Well. Who's for
lunch?"

Her group had already doffed their rucksacks, lining
them up on a fallen log that made a handy woodsy
pantry, and cans of lemonade and root beer had been
set in the trickle of a stream to chill. While the two
older girls (who called each other Mindy and Kathy)
unpacked the rucksack lunches, the two younger ones
gathered a small pile of flat stones, cleared away a large
fallen branch from the open space near Miss Bostweiler's rock, and spread out the old green-and-white
checked tablecloth that always came on Sierra Club out-
ings in Miss B.'s pack basket. The stones went to hold
down the corners. A moment later a small boy staggered into view, weighed down by a large and mossy
rock. "Table decoration," he wheezed, and dropped
the rock in the middle of the cloth. "There were some

wild roses, but you said not to pick flowers," he explained earnestly.

"Oh, Ernie, you've got your jeans *filthy*," said Kathy in a tone that only a sister would use.

"Doesn't matter. Good work, Ernie." Miss Bostweiler got down on her hands and knees to peer at the rock, though she must have been old enough to be everyone's grandmother. "It looks like a miniature forest up close, doesn't it? You've got one, two . . . three kinds of moss there. See the orange and lemony spots? They're lichen."

"Moss is pretty," agreed one of the younger girls. "But can you eat it?"

"I don't know about these, Marnie, but there *are* edible mosses. They boil down into a sort of gelatin. Taste as blah as plain gelatin, too, but with blackberries and sugar and cream, you might be able to whip up a nice mousse. That's a pudding, not a moose," she said sternly, before Ernie could open his mouth. She stood. "Where'd Barney get to?"

"Coming!" A boy's voice rang out not far away, and in a moment the boy himself pushed through the dense grove of hemlocks up to their right. "I got us some plates." He waved a handful of large maple leaves, some of them ten inches across. "Once you get through those old hemlocks, the woods aren't so thick. There are some big old maples and a bunch of locust trees."

Miss Bostweiler frowned as she set the leaf plates around the cloth. "Locusts? Up here? Good grief, whose sandwich is *this*? Squashed plastic bread and peanut butter with purple jelly dribbling out on all sides!" She held a waxed-paper sandwich bag out at arm's length and made a dreadful face.

"Mine," said Ernie Goble sheepishly. "I like squishy bread."

Miss Bostweiler regarded him with pity. "Do you? It seems a waste of good peanut butter and jelly, but I suppose you know what you like. I expect you'll grow out of it. Squishy bread is only good for making bread pills, and I grew out of *them* when I was eight."

Ernie was relieved. "I'm only seven," he said thankfully, and licked off the jelly drips before putting the sandwich on his maple leaf.

The lunch came together like a happy jigsaw puzzle. Out of the pack basket came a wonderfully thin wooden bowl, a thick wad of nasturtium and borage leaves tied with a piece of grass, and a little bottle of oil and vinegar dressing. Each of the knapsacks furnished something more for the salad, and Miss Bostweiler listened with interest to the explanation of each addition: basil and tiny cherry tomatoes young Marnie and her friend (whose name appeared to be Courtney Moll) had raised in flowerpots; home-grown chives and green onions from the Moll garden; eggs laid by Goble chickens and hard-boiled by Kathy; and a handful of watercress Barney had harvested in the shallows down where the creek ran alongside the long-forgotten road. Ernie's contribution was a small flat tin of anchovies. "I *like* salty things," he said apologetically.

"Perfect." Miss Bostweiler nodded briskly.

"But you said we ought to find the lunch things in our gardens or in the woods," Kathy objected. "Ernie never gets *any*thing right."

Miss Bostweiler peeled two green beech twigs to toss the salad with. "Nonsense. At least he knows what stores are for. I suppose you could grow peanuts and do your own peanut butter, but you don't see anchovies in Pennsylvania creeks. Now, the bowls."

The salad bowls lined up on the log were battered tin cups and plastic Speedi-Whip cartons and bowls neatly cut from the bottoms of the largest sort of plastic bottles. "Why buy new when this'll do?" seemed to be Miss Bostweiler's motto. "Money's for buying the good and beautiful things you can't make for yourself," she said, as she uncorked her bottle of homemade root beer and took a long cool swallow. "Now," said Miss B., when it came time to slice the spice cake that had nestled in her basket under the salad bowl. "Down to club business. Who's got George Washington's letter?"

"Me." Mindy Hallam pulled a wrinkled scrap of paper from her jeans pocket. "I copied it out from Marnie's daddy's copy."

"Mmm." Miss B. licked a smear of icing from her thumb. "Where's that bit about . . . oh, here: . . . *which Road, affording an Easie Progress across the Mountain, provides the Forts a Speedie Access the one to the other, and spanning this Wilderness, joins our two High Wayes, a Circumstance adventitious both to Communication and to Commerce.* Mmph. We are on the wrong track. If G.W. says 'commerce,' he means wagons."

"But this was a road, down below," objected Barney. "Just because it was washed out doesn't mean it couldn't've been a good road once."

"Daddy says the creek's been called Old Way Creek as far back as all the Mosstown maps and records go," put in Kathy Goble. "This has just *got* to be George Washington's lost road. Hasn't it?"

Miss Bostweiler shook her head. "That bit of road

peters out at the bottom of this gully. It could have been an old mining or logging track. . . ." Her brows drew together in a faint frown. "I had an idea there was a farm up this way, back when I was a girl, but it must've been further north. What *is* sure is that not even an ox team could get a wagon over the ridge by the route they're scouting up above." She tapped her map. "This little run comes from a spring a few hundred yards above us, and it looks as if the hill climbs even more steeply above that. No, let's us try for another stream. Over that way." She nodded toward the screen of hemlocks. "We can clean up, explore in that direction, and be back before the others have finished their nut bars and raisins and headed back down again."

While the utensils were being rinsed and the cloth folded, the three boys took the empty soft drink cans and searched out two large flat rocks for can smashers. They took turns teeter-tottering until all they had was a handful of tidy tin pancakes, which were then stowed in a knapsack. Only the leaf plates were left, and the cake crumbs for the birds.

"Right." Miss B. pulled on an ancient straw hat and began counting noses. "Hallam, Goble one, Goble two, two Molls, and one Willis. . . . Where *is* Willis?"

"She was right behind me." Courtney Moll looked around anxiously. "Marn?"

Everyone called. "Mar-nee!"

After a moment's silence, there was a breathless shriek from a little way down the hill. "Coming. I *found* something."

As they waited, Ernie suddenly gave Miss B.'s hand a tug. "Miss Bostweiler? If we do find George Washington's lost road, what do we do with it? Whose will it be? Finders-keepers?" Always earnest, Ernie scowled more somberly than ever.

His sister, who always knew everything, put in, "Daddy says the bottom part belongs to one of the farms down below. You know, the old Warnecki place. It used to be called Sampson's, and before that, Inkle's Springs. But we don't know the people who live there now."

Miss B. frowned. "I wish I could remember the name of the people who lived up the hill from them. Something Scottish, it was. The old man was just the sort of pinched-up miser who'd fence off his part of a road and charge hikers a fifty-cent toll. If he's still alive, he'll probably set up a roadside stand and cut down all the trees to make wooden plates with *Souveneer of the George Washinton Rode* stamped on 'em in runny purple ink." She snorted at the thought. "I suppose he'd be a hundred by now, so he's probably dead. You're right, though, young Ernest. Preserving a road isn't easy. We protect animals and can try to save the rare ones by raising more in a zoo, but it's different with plants and trees and roads if somebody greedy owns 'em. They just aren't movable. All our group could do would be to try to get the state to declare it a Historical Monument or to buy it up for a state park."

"If it was mine, *I'd* save it," Ernie said. "I'd fix it, and have wagons to ride people up it. With oxes to pull them."

"Oxen," corrected Mindy in a strangled voice, as Marnie joined the others. "Gosh, *look*."

"Yes, look what I found!" Marnie thrust out her hand.

In the middle of her small palm sat Pete's tiny lunch basket, perfectly made, and no more than an inch high. The children in their amazement missed the odd look of mingled shock and excitement that flashed across Miss Bostweiler's face.

"*That's* finder's-keeper's, isn't it?" asked Ernie.

"What?" said Miss B. vaguely. "Er, yes, I suppose it is. Here, Marnie dear." She handed it back with a thoughtful frown. "Odd. Very odd. It's absolutely perfect." She chewed thoughtfully at her lip. "Can you show us where you found it?"

In a moment Miss Bostweiler and the children were off down the hillside at an easy pace that left Pete hurrying far behind. He had missed his chance. He should have shown himself. For years he had hoped to find as sensible a person as Miss Bostweiler, but long isolation and the habit of mistrust rose up to hold him still and silent in the laurel shadows. Only as the last of the children had disappeared had the spell broken.

Belle!

Pete put on a burst of speed, bounding and slithering down the leaf-matted forest slope. He had left old Belle with the lunch and his gun—but the small girl had found only the basket. Why only that? If she had tipped it over with her foot, it might have spilled its contents and rolled away, but now. . . . *Just don't you bark, old girl,* Pete prayed. *Leastwise not till I get there.*

Ahead, Miss Bostweiler's voice rang out. "No, it's a pretty toy, but there's no sign of who dropped it." She seemed to hesitate, but then announced briskly. "I don't think we'll take the time to explore beyond Barney's hemlocks after all. We passed a pool on White Oak Creek that looked a perfect place for trout, and I'd like to have another look. Have any of you ever tried to catch a trout by tickling it? No? Well, come along then."

They were gone before Pete came puffing up. Where was Belle? If they hadn't found her, where *was* she? Pete looked around frantically. If she'd been stepped on, it was all his fault. . . .

"*Belle!*" he yelled.

A thankful *Bow-roo!* answered.

Belle sat, shaking, but as firmly as if she had been planted, next to the young oak tree where he had left her. The spilled lunch, the sack of May apples, and his rifle had been tidied into a neat pile, and both these and the dog had been hidden beneath a broad maple leaf. The leaf had been propped against the tree trunk to make a shady lean-to.

Eleven

PETE HAD NO RECOLLECTION OF THE TRIP HOME, BUT since he was there, he reckoned he must have come. And no one had followed, or they'd have turned up before now. He lifted the pot from the stove and shakily poured himself a cup of coffee.

"Well, Belle," he said, drinking off the portion that had sloshed into the saucer, "you ain't the only one." Old Belle lay on the faded hooked rug beside the stove, still trembling with excitement. She had never before been so close to human beings—except Pete, of course, but that was different.

Pete frowned into his cup. It was the last of Granny's "chiney" ones, and he never used it except on Thanksgiving and Christmas and Decoration Day, yet here he was, having plain old coffee in it on an ordinary Saturday, as if the whole world had been stood on its ear. That lost road, now . . . could the old farm road once have been a part of it? Long ago there had been a faint grassy trace running on from where the road ended by the orchard. Might still be. Some of the trees up that way were old as old. Think of it! *George Washington*. He might have surveyed the old road in the first place.

But Pete's awe faded into worry as he remembered the talk of Historical Monuments and State Parks. The woods would be full of outlandish folk tramping down ferns and nosing in where they weren't wanted. The skinny woman in short trousers—Miss Bostweiler? —seemed sensible enough and likely to be sympathetic, but Pete had lost his chance to enlist her help. An invasion of curious strangers would mean the end of the farm. Pete sank back in Granny's old rocker with a queasy feeling in the pit of his stomach.

The coffee wasn't much help, china cup or no. It was made from ground-up roasted dandelion roots, and though Granny always claimed that of all her coffee recipes it came closest to the real thing, Pete wished he'd brewed a pan of wild mint tea instead. Only after a thick slab of bread spread with sweet butter and bramble jelly did his frown smooth away. "Wish I had some of that peanut butter," he sighed. "I forgot there was such a thing. Beech-Nut Peanut Butter, it was." But wishing buttered no parsnips and moaning didn't mow the grass, as Granny had recorded in the Book. He'd done without peanut butter for fifty years, and he could manage without it now. He cut another thick slice of bread.

"Wish I could recollect who that woman puts me in mind of," he muttered. "Mighty strange rig she was wearing. Granny'd've had a conniption fit if she knew

(104)

ladies had come to trottin' around with their knees
uncovered. Miss Bostweiler, the little fellow called
her. We never knowed no Bostweilers. *Any* Bostweilers," he amended guiltily. His grammar had gone
sadly to seed since Granny died. He reached a little
mirror down from the wall. "Reckon I could use a
trim, too. Anybody saw me now'd take me for some
new kind of furry creeter for sure." Carefully, with a
delicate old pair of embroidery scissors, he snipped here
and there and back again until the gingery bush became a trim moustache and short full beard. His hair

at the back was a trifle long for warm weather, so he hacked that off too, with the kitchen shears.

Cheered by his new smartness, Pete set about his neglected chores, fetching the little jar of sourdough starter from the cool springhouse and mixing up a batch of birch-bread dough that could rise while he weeded the pepper patch and then sprayed the apple and plum trees with the Mixture. The fruit was setting up nicely, but there were, as always, a pestiferous lot of insects to discourage. Pulling on the old gloves he always wore when working with the Mixture, he measured out ground-up red peppers and ground shallots and garlic, and crumbled a handful of dried tansy leaves to dust. Mixed into a paste with warm water, and stirred into a bucket of cold water, the ingredients were set aside to soak while he weeded and mulched. There was a lot of weeding and mulching to do. The pepper patch had grown almost as big as the rest of the vegetable garden together. It seemed that the more corn and tomatoes and cabbages the humus-rich earth produced, the more pests heard about it, and the more Pete had to take after them with the peppery spray. Last winter he got the old forge going and made a new and bigger sprayer out of a small steel drum, the wheels from a child's velocipede, and some odds and ends of scrap iron from old Trashbin's junk collection.

"Everything was coming right along, and now them hikers are like to stick a spoke in it," Pete grieved, heading out into the sunshine with Belle at his heels. "Even the strawberries is doing right nice, now we get enough marigold seeds every year to plant amongst the berries. Marigolds stop them dad-ratted little root nibblers coming in, just like Granny always said." He eyed the old dog gloomily. " 'Course, seeing as how the varmints got Nell's last litter of pups, and young Fetch had to get himself tromped on by a dumb plowing steer, it looks like I'll have to get along without a dog after you and Nell pass on. But everything else is holding together, I reckon. We're *never* like to run out of cats. That Melindy and Tibby and Emma surely do run themselves a kitten factory."

"Now why—" he said, stopping short and leaning on his hoe. "Now why do you s'pose that Bettwhistler female steered them folks back down to the South Fork after all that talk about coming along thisaway? It does beat all why she'd shear off and point 'em south instead of up this way, like she was gonter."

The uneasiness hung over him the rest of the afternoon. If "thet female" knew there had once been a farm above the old Sampson place at Inkle's Springs, she ought to have guessed that it would have been built on the old road over the ridge. By all rights, pure female curiosity should have sent her north to the wide gentle bowl in the hillside that still sheltered the farm. The little girl's discovery of the tiny lunch basket could have put everything else out of Miss Bett —Bostweiler's head. But then there was the matter of that basket. By all rights a queer little thing like that should have set off a treasure hunt.

"There you go again, Pete. Looking gift horses in the mouth. They're gone fer now, and naught else matters. Ain't that right, old girl?" Pete dipped a pail of water from the spring to rinse out the sprayer.

Belle barked, a short sharp *yip* that Pete took for an

answer. But Belle's daughter Nell caught the urgent note of that yip and arrived in a headlong rush from the other side of the barn. Pete, unmindful of their ruckus, trundled the sprayer off to the toolshed with never a look behind.

Belle was beside herself. It wasn't like Pete to miss a danger sign or turn his back on a friend's warning. She and Nell circled the spring, growling, their hackles bristling, but there was only the one footprint, smack in the middle of the mud and as big around as the print left by the springhouse pail. With claws. The scent was overpowering. The dogs whimpered, tucked their tails between their legs, and skittered after Pete.

The alarm was not slow in spreading. Passing the old chicken coop, the dogs barked at Emma, sunning on the doorstep. Emma shot inside, making for a nest among the towering stacks of moldy *Ladies' Home Journals*, *Country Gentlemans*, and *The Poultryman's Periodicals*. Snatching an indignant kitten by the scruff of its neck, she trotted off to the barn and raced back for another. By the time the fifth and last was safe in the stall with Tibby's litter, the cows were lowing, the steers stamping, the two bulls bellowing, and the chickens fluttering in a panic that would put them off laying eggs for days.

"Now, what in tarnation set *you* all off?" said Pete, when he came in to milk the cows. As his strong gentle fingers stripped the milk into the wooden pails, he sang, starting on Bossie with "A Tavern in the Town," going through "Barb'ry Allen," "There's a Hole in My Bucket," and "Adeline," to end up on Flora with Granny's favorite, "I Walked in the Garden Alone."

"It's not a psalm," Granny had taken pains to explain, "nor a hymn, exactly. So the good Lord knows I mean no disrespect when I sing it out of church, jes' to the chickens and the good blue sky." By the second chorus, with its booming lilt, the bulls—Moose and Durham —had settled down. Even Belle and Nell, sharing a pannikin of milk, decided the world might be right-side-up after all.

An hour after dark, when old Belle had settled down to a dream of chasing weasels, she was rudely roused by Pete's starting up in bed to exclaim, "By gosh . . . *little Samantha Bostweiler!* That's who she is. LITTLE Samantha! Same laugh, same . . . but how in tarnation *could* it be? Unless old Professor Lilliput put things right for them Dopple folks after all." A crazy hope flared briefly and then died. "It ain't likely. Not a mean old cuss like him." Pete sank back into his feather pillows with a sigh. "Mebbe it ain't Samantha. Some kin of hers, more like." Even if she *were* little Samantha, little Samantha quite probably knew nothing of the Professor's assault on the sleeping farm. But —surely she would remember that long-ago Petey?

"Nope. It ain't atall likely. Not after all these years." He yawned and stretched out to his full six inches. "Such a long time," he whispered.

Old Belle clambered onto the bed and wriggled up until her head was on a pillow too. For once, Pete let her stay.

Twelve

IN THE MIDDLE OF THE NIGHT, FROM THE COMFORTABLE deepness between dreams, Pete was suddenly plunged into wakefulness by Belle's frantic whimpers and long wet tongue. At first he pretended to be asleep, but when, standing on his chest, she leaned down to bark in his ear, he sighed and gave up.

"What is it, old girl? Oh, git down, for Pete's sake!" Belle, in great agitation, ran to the open window, then came back to tug at the tail of Pete's nightshirt.

"Awright, awright," he grumbled. One bony foot flapped along the floor, found a pair of quilted carpet slippers, and dragged them close. Shod and with a patchwork flannel sheet over his shoulders, he scuffed to the window to see what could have put old Belle in such a state.

The back garden sloped away to the barn: silver-bleached grass, shadowy rosebushes and hydrangeas, their blooms smudges of black wine and silver in the moonlight. Belle whined.

"Hush, I'm looking, ain't I?" Pete raised the squeaky window sash the rest of the way and leaned out.

Nothing. Not a cat on a middle-night prowl or the trampling rustle of deer shifting bed places. The barn, a pale and sagging hulk, hung against its background of dark trees as if it had been pinned there to prevent its falling down. Another blizzard as heavy as March of '72, and it just might.

"Old girl," said Pete, drawing in his head. "You bin dreaming."

Belle trembled against his knee, and as he reached out toward the sash, suddenly shoved in front of him. On her hind legs, forepaws on the sill, she set up an angry frightened barking. With scarcely a breath between, she barked and barked and barked.

"I declare, dog! There ain't no varmints out there. They're too feared of the deer to come in. Now, git out of the way 'fore I shut the window on you. You—"

A heavy, breathy hiss answered Belle's frantic scolding.

Belle, hearing, scrambled under the bed.

Pete swallowed nervously. Trying not to put his weight on the creaky middle floorboard, he gingerly edged out for another look.

The hiss came again, deep and close by, the sound of a wary animal breathing threats. Pete looked straight down onto a long, furry back.

The weasel—it was a weasel—slid around the corner of the house like a ripple of brown fog. It was not as huge as it might have been, being young, but that was quite huge enough.

The old shotgun was not in its corner. "Drat!" Pete

thought, easing the window down. "Them blamed hikers been too much on my mind. First time in years I forgot the blamed thing, too." He gave Belle a quick pat, laid a warning finger aside her nose, and tiptoed across the creaky floor to the stairway.

Following the wall in the pitch-black hall, Pete made it to the kitchen and the shotgun propped in the corner by the back door. Rummaging along an overhead shelf for the cigar box with the shells—he had had to learn to make his own—he found it between a sackful of bottle caps and an iron-hard loaf of bread that he had put up out of mouse reach and forgotten.

The shotgun broke with a well-oiled *snick!* Old Pete slipped two of the pepper-filled shells into the chambers and *snicked* it shut again. Buckshot wasn't any use against the big varmints. Besides being a nuisance to make, what with melting down the lead and all, it just bounced off their hides or itched like a bit of sand in an eye. But the pepper, with luck—the wind being right—could send an unwelcome visitor growling off to bathe his eyes or give him such a fit of sneezing that his nose wouldn't know a cow from a currant bush for days.

Sidling up to the kitchen sink, Pete leaned over and undid the window catch. The window went up with a faint *scree!*, but when Pete nerved himself to look out, there was nothing. Down beyond the roses and vegetables, the barn still slept. The varmint had to be circling the house still, trying warily to puzzle out the man-and-dog smell. Now, if it would only oblige by poking its face in at the window. . . . Pete's face creased with a grin.

In the furthest corner of the kitchen the butt end of a honey-cured ham hung from a rafter hook. With a silent chuckle, Pete laid the shotgun on the kitchen table and fetched a chair to stand on. Unhooked and unwrapped, the ham smelled sweet and smoky. Pete cut two thick slices and a thin one, setting the ham itself in the sink and the two slices on the windowsill. He shared the thin slice with Belle, then moved the table back, to give himself a clear shot.

Nothing.

The ham seemed to need a little help, so Pete let out a high, nasal *ske-e-e!* he hoped might pass for a mouse in terror. *Ske-e-e!*

The weasel, unfortunately, was crouched directly below the window at the first *skee*, and by the second had raised its nose into ham-range and with a graceful swoop of a snaky neck had scooped up slices, ham and all. By the time the shotgun came up to Pete's eye, the varmint's nose was well outside again.

"I'll be ding-donged if I'm gonter give you another one o' them hams," Pete muttered. He fired both barrels.

The concussion brought the sash rattling down—but not before some, at least, of the pepper had puffed out the window, for the weasel's sneeze blew out two panes loosened by the crash.

"Criminentlies!" exclaimed Pete in disgust, and then "Ka-*choo!*" He hastily covered his nose and mouth with a patchwork flannel tea towel and with another tried to flap the drifting powdered pepper toward the broken window.

Outside, there was another fierce sneeze, and the

paw that had come dabbling in at one hole was hastily withdrawn. *Khwa-hschee!* The furious weasel raised up on its hind legs and slanted a parting swipe at the offending window, then turned to stumble blindly toward the barn, shaking its head as if it hoped to shake the pepper out. Pete was left staring at the gaping hole behind the sink.

"Dad-blasted four-legged sneak!" Pete snatched his granddaddy's long rifle down from its pegs above the door and, as the nightshirt had no pockets, dragged on his jacket and filled the pockets with shells and cartridges. He slammed out the back door carrying both guns. Belle, sensibly, stayed behind to lick the ham wrappings.

For the weasel, crashing into the barn was the last straw. Red-eyed, tender-nosed, confused and enraged, it reared up to its considerable length and bit the barn. The corner post, a good foot (by the farm's standards) in diameter, having quietly rotted loose under the eaves, sprang free of the roof corner under this attack. The siding boards screeched in protest, then sprang back with a dull *spwa-a-ck!* Mortar sifted from the stone walls of the lower floor. The roof groaned down to a deep sag and then held.

For a moment there was astonished silence. Then the ruckus began. The screeching, bawling, bleating stock had caught a musky whiff of weasel, and the weasel had caught a weak whiff of them. Watery nose or no, he sensed a meal more succulent even than the ham appetizer. He rooted at the stone wall.

Pete had gained the cover of the outhouse and from there slipped to the toolshed, which was as close as he could safely get. Trembling with haste, he loaded the shotgun with one pepper shell and one buckshot, edged to the corner, and took sight. The corner of the barn was a good twenty yards away—too far for pepper—but Pete was counting on the bang to attract the beast's attention. If only his hands would steady down, he could then try for one good rifle shot. It went against the grain, killing varmints—"wasting God's critters," Granny had called it—but considerably less so when the varmint was near wasting six cows, three steers, two bulls, twelve pigs, six sheep, thirty-eight chickens, thirteen cats, and Belle's Nell.

But the weasel was young, and Pete over sixty. The spattering of fine buckshot brought that lean length down to a crouch in the dusty road. While Pete was bringing the rifle up, the weasel was deciding that, human smell or no, Pete would make an acceptable second *hors d'oeuvre.*

Pete hadn't a hope, but he ran anyway. The weasel, thinking perhaps to drive him toward the barn and make him part of a general feast, streaked the long way around the toolshed, a maneuver that required rapid, smooth cornering, and did not allow for the booby-trapped vegetable garden. One foot tangled fast in the rope-and-wire netting, setting up a musical jangle of jugs, tin cans, and broken bottle necks.

The clank and confusion did not gain Pete much time, but at least it looked like gaining him the flimsy protection of the long rose arbor for the last sprint to the house. The weasel came after, sounding like a wedding party speeding headlong to the reception dinner. Sure that he felt the hot breath on the back of his new-trimmed neck, Pete put on an extra burst of speed.

Yards (or rather, inches) from the arbor, with a dreadful pain in his side and his heart *thonk*ing in his ears, Pete heard an indignant, squealing gasp, a whoosh, and a great, tinkling crash. Broken glass pattered on the rose leaves.

A voice, dimly familiar, came from a most alarming direction: *up*.

"I got him," it said. "At least, I *think* I got him. I'd better go chuck him off in the woods in case he's not dead. Even if he wakes up, he'll sure stay clear of here." There was a pause, what sounded like a yawn, then, " 'Course, that doesn't matter now."

That doesn't matter now? A bewildered Pete Mac-Cubbin crept to the south side of the arbor and parted the leaves. He chewed his lip unhappily at what he saw. The weasel had come in because the deer had moved out, and he was looking at the reason why.

Smack in the middle of a south field trampled beyond repair stood the boy Ernie, who had been with the hiking party. In one hand he held a heavy stick. From the other, clutched by the tail, dangled the unconscious weasel, bottles and all.

"I left my sleeping bag out there in the grass," said Ernie to the rose arbor in general. "I'll be back in the morning when I can see where to step." Whereupon he brushed between two maples in the far fencerow as if they were saplings and disappeared like a giant in a dream.

That doesn't matter now. For the rest of the night Pete tossed and twisted, unable to sleep, fretting about what the boy could have meant. For all his being what seemed to Pete forty or so feet tall, he *was* only a child. Seven? Eight? Where had he come from? Were the others camped out in the tall grass too? Or had the boy run away from home? Almost everybody thought about running away from home, from what Pete remembered, but they hardly ever did it. Not without making sure somebody saw them packing the suitcase and heading down the road. By breakfast time Pete still had not slept.

The boy had come *here*. Not away from, but to. Pete's stomach fluttered uneasily. Not even an extravagant breakfast of garlic sausages, six eggs sunny-side up, sourdough biscuits with butter and wild honey and May-apple marmalade settled it down. Every two minutes he was up and peering out the shattered window across the mangled south field. The queasy feeling sent him at last to the store cupboard under the stairs for a soothing sip of black currant cordial.

Not even a tumblerful of cordial could have eased the shock of the sight that met him on returning to the window. *The boy was kneeling at the damaged corner of the barn. He had picked off the broken bits of siding, and was reaching down through the loft, lifting out pig after pig, stowing them in a cigar box.*

"Now, just a darned minute," roared Pete. He hadn't spoken to another human being in twenty-five years, but he almost made up for lost time in sheer volume. *"YOU CAN'T DO THAT!"*

Ernie jumped guiltily. At the sight of Pete, he gave a cheerful "Phew!" Tenderly depositing the first of the sheep among the hysterical pigs, he offered a shy, excited smile. " 'Morning. I'm Ernie Goble."

"I don't give a hoot who you are," Pete raged. "You keep your hands offen my livestock. Lookit that stupid ewe, you bird-witted infant. She's throwing herself a fit."

The wild-eyed ewe sheep was, indeed, gasping and heaving in a sort of asthmatic fit. Stricken, Ernie drew his hand away as Pete climbed into the box, pushed the ewe over on her side, and sat on her until she could scarcely breathe at all. He then slipped off and rhythmically pressed the well-padded ribs to get her going right. "Just what in . . . blue blazes . . . do you think . . . you're doing . . . Mister Ernie Goble?"

"I only—well, I *was* going to pack straw in between them so they wouldn't slide around. I made airholes, too." He pointed hopefully to four small perforations in the box lid. "My sister's got these two dollhouses she doesn't use anymore, and I thought the old beat-up one could be your barn. Nobody goes out in the garden shed where they're at, so you'd be safe, you see."

Pete stared. *"Safe?"*

The boy watched anxiously as Pete moved among the pigs, calming them with a word here and a slap on the rump there.

"I suppose," said Ernie doubtfully, "I could come back and fetch your house if I brought my old wagon. If my Mom doesn't shut me in my room for coming up here last night when I was supposed to be at my aunt's. But your barn's as tall as I am. *Nobody* could carry it."

"Nobody asked you to," Pete snapped. Stepping over

(118)

the rim of the box, he moved to the side barn door. "You just slide that pen of yours over here so's I can put my animals back where they belong." He jerked the wooden pin free of the hasp and swung the door open, ducking the attack of the bantam rooster who flapped out, spurs forward, ready to defend the barn to the death.

"It's him you want, not me," Pete observed sourly, but at the sight of the boy the rooster reconsidered and stalked off, making a great show of hunting for beetles.

Pete tilted his head back to yell up to the boy. "What in tarnation are you waiting for? I said shove that box over here. And I'll want a word with you after. Now the farm's found, I need to write a couple letters, and you kin take 'em along to Mosstown for me. It's Mosstown you're from, ain't it? Well, these letters is important. You'll have to get your Paw to deliver 'em to Judge Hesselbein, Parson Knott, and the sheriff. And one for Sam—er, for Miss Bostweiler, too."

Young Ernie brushed all that aside. "You don't understand. You won't need any letters." He spoke slowly and carefully, as if Mr. MacCubbin were not very bright; as if he were some sort of hairless and superior squirrel rather than a fellow human being. "I'm *rescuing* you. Saturday, lots of people are coming up here to look for George Washington's road, and if they find you, the old man that owns this place'll put you all in cages and charge people for looks."

"*I'm* the old man that owns this place," raged Pete, but the boy went on doggedly.

"That's why I've got to move you, see? So I can

'preserve you in your Natural Habitat.' Or anyhow, as close as I can fix it," he amended. He frowned. "Besides, the Judge's name is Stover."

Pete froze. Of course. Saying "when we get word to Mosstown" had become such a habit that both he and Granny had long ago fallen into the error of fancying that the world outside stood still. And, of course, it didn't. If Samantha and he had their gray hairs, the others were probably all dead and gone, like Granny: Judge Hesselbein, Miss Ample, Parson Knott, and—*and Professor Lilliput.* Pete reached out a hand to the barn door to steady himself as his head whirled.

The Reducer! By now it must be rusted away on some deserted dump. Unless . . . ! Little Samantha had mentioned a nephew whom neither Trashbin nor Pete had ever seen, and if he were still around, he *might* still have the Reducer. Or know where it was. *Must* know, or how else had Samantha been unshrunk? Still, that might have happened years ago.

"Here, now! What the ding-dong do you think you're at?" Pete jerked back to the present problem just as the boy was depositing two lambs and an astonished Nell in the cigar box. "What ails you, boy? You *deef?*"

Ignoring Pete's protests as placidly as if he were indeed deaf, the boy Ernie stood, brushed off the knees of his jeans, and calmly pried up the sagging barn roof. Straining, he managed to fold it back like a lid, whereupon it ripped loose of its own weight and toppled with a crash into the road on the downhill side. He peered inside.

"I don't know about the chickens," Ernie said

slowly. "I should've brought another little box. But I've got two good deep ones for the cows and you. I saw you in the woods, you know, and I guessed from the dog that you'd have more animals. And I thought you'd have stuff you'd like to bring along so the new place'd feel more like home. Furniture maybe. I'll go get the boxes. They're in my pack basket."

He stepped over the old chicken coop, crossed the south field, and disappeared through the trees.

Pete looked after the boy helplessly, desperately. He hauled Nell and the sheep and lambs out of the box and climbed in to corner the pigs and tip them out, but, this done, he wavered uncertainly in the dusty yard.

What next? Where did you hide with—*how* did you hide with six cows, three steers, two bulls, twelve pigs, six sheep, thirty-eight chickens, thirteen cats, and two dogs?

Thirteen

THE BED CREAKED AS PETE TURNED RESTLESSLY, BURYING his nose in the pillow. He dreamed that he was raising the barn roof with a rope and block and tackle. Every time it was ready to drop into place, the wind tipped it over again, *phwumph*! He was whipped aloft at the end of the rope and falling. . . .

Flailing bedclothes in all directions, Pete jerked up, beard bristling and ears ringing. It was a moment before he realized that he had not been flung over the barn onto his head, and another before his ears stopped ringing. Then he remembered the boy Ernie and padded to the window. A gray glimmer showed through the trees down east of the barn. Not 5:30 yet. Nothing stirred. He drew a chair up to the window and sat watching until a cock halfheartedly crowed. One of the dogs wuffed in answer from the back porch. Like any other day. Pete shivered in his patchwork nightshirt. It was bound to be like no other day at all.

The stalemate could not last. The boy would be hungry and impatient and not likely to be put off again by Pete's bluff that he would shoot the stock before he would let them be "some kid's bitty private sideshow." Even if it hadn't been a bluff, the boy had only to stick Pete in his pocket and load up his boxes in peace.

The dogs whined at the back door. Pete stood, slowly, feeling for the first time all sixty-two of his years. "Brain too stiff and creaky to figure a way out," he grumbled. "Comes of havin' every day pretty much the same as every other, I reckon." Lifting the heavy pitcher on the washstand, he sloshed water into the china basin and had a good wash.

"Just when things *was* goin' a bit better, too," he spluttered. There hadn't been a shred of towel for years, so he dried on a piece of old chenille bedspread, dressed, and tramped downstairs.

A scratching, whining, and meowing set up on the back porch as soon as Pete reached the kitchen. Unbolting the door, he found Belle and Nell and all thirteen cats, including four so little that they still had the staggers when they tried to walk. In they crowded, with a great show of rubbing against his feet and ankles. Clearly they knew something was up. "No use lookin' to me," Pete said sourly.

A number of paws were trod upon as Pete moved about the kitchen, cleaning out the stove, laying and lighting the fire, and cutting bacon and bread. "What d'you think you are? A gol-durned ankle muff?" Losing his patience, Pete lifted his foot and shook Emma loose. He had never seen cats so nervously affectionate.

Emma shifted her attentions to Belle, who looked considerably startled but made no objection.

As a precaution before going down to the barn for eggs and milk, Pete stuck the plate of bread and bacon on a high shelf. Then he took up a basket and went out to look at the morning, thinking it might well be his last chance. He had to keep a sharp eye out for any sign of the boy Ernie too and so did not notice how oddly the porch roof sagged, and almost missed seeing that the steps had unaccountably disappeared, but caught himself in time and stepped down carefully. The dogs and cats followed, with the kittens being ferried down in relays.

"Something spook you, eh?" In the barn, sitting beside Bossie, Pete relented and scratched ears all around. After the milking he set out pans of warm milk garnished with raw egg, but though Belle and Nell lapped greedily, the cats only twitched their tails, wailed softly, and crowded underfoot again. Pete began to be uneasy in the roofless barn. Even the bulls were subdued, snuffling and turning in their high-walled stalls. Pete noticed that the split logs he had used to mend Moose's gate and wall the month before had disappeared. Odd . . . but it scarcely mattered, with things as bad as they were.

On the way back to the house he was too heavy-hearted to give more than a passing glance to the collapsed tangle of roses that had been the extension of the arbor or the holes that pocked the house roof. The cats sat in the barn door and wailed for him to come back. But Pete, with an uneasy look around for the boy, kept on, climbing onto the porch with a frown for the missing steps.

Belle growled in her throat and clambered up after him. She was eleven, and it was an awkward scramble, but her hackles were up and her teeth bared.

Pete stopped cold.

That smell!

The aromas that floated out the door were . . . bacon, yes, but that other—rich, dark, mouth-watering? "Coffee!" whispered Pete incredulously. Memories of Granny swam before his eyes: Granny standing at the kitchen table, holding the coffee grinder, while a small Petey cranked away at the handle. *Real* coffee, freshly ground. Not dandelion roots, roasted brown and boiled up in a saucepan.

Belle growled again, menacingly, and Pete woke from his trance. Warily, he sidled up to the door and leaned in for a look.

A thin woman with short-cropped hair and a calico smock stood draining fat from the bacon pan into the old chipped crock. On the stove the glass knob on top of Granny's good enamel coffeepot glowed and burped. There was a fresh cloth on the table, and a place was laid with the last good bits of china.

Pete swallowed, cleared his throat, and still could manage only a bewildered croak. "Wh-who . . ."

The woman turned, fork in hand, to stare at him with open curiosity. "Peter MacCubbin!" she said softly, taking in with a shrewd eye the lanky figure, the china-blue eyes in the weather-brown face, and the trim ginger beard. "I expect you don't remember me."

Pete cleared his throat more firmly. "You're Samantha. *Little* Samantha . . . ain't you? I seen you in the woods Saturday. But how—" He darted a bewildered look out the door. "How's come you ain't, uh, *taller?* You ain't been shrunk again . . . ?" He suddenly had a horrid vision of generation after generation of Kurtzes reducing patches of Pennsylvania willy-nilly until—

"No, no!" Samantha, reading his look, grinned, shaking her head. "Everything's been put right. *You've* been put right."

The laugh and the gesture were so like his memory of the tiny Samantha that the incredible began to be merely astonishing. He sat down abruptly. "I don't understand a bit of it. Not a danged bit."

"It's all very simple." Samantha broke four eggs into the skillet. "The Professor died, his nephew was caught, and we were all unshrunk. The Reducer's being perfected by MBM—Mammoth Business Machines—and it's being kept pretty top secret, but it has brought your farm back to its old self with very few people the wiser. We headed off the search party that was out looking for young Ernie Goble, and when we found him, he was carried down the ridge—in the middle of the night, this was—sound asleep. By now he must be awake and wondering if it was all a dream."

She dished up the eggs and bacon and quickly fried a slice of bread. "As soon as I saw that little basket of yours, I *knew*. Well, anyway, as soon as I saw your old dog trying to look like a dead mouseling. I covered him up and hurried the children away and then later, when I'd pieced together what must have happened, I got busy on the telephone. It took a bit of doing, but MBM finally agreed to fly the latest model of the Reducer in from St. Louis . . . and there you are."

"Just like that," said Pete.

"Yes," said Samantha. "Now, what *I* want to know is how you cured that bacon. Honey, I know, but I can't place that heavenly smell. Is it herbs or the wood you use to smoke it? Here, have some of the coffee I brought."

Pete, his world upended, found himself answering questions about recipes and wild vegetables. It was probably just as well. Too many answers crowding upon the questions that tumbled in his head, and he might have grown more frightened than amazed. As it was, he had a fleeting urge to nip off into the woods with the dogs while Samantha's back was turned. Living off chickweed and peppergrass might be better than going out into a strange, changed world where you didn't know a soul.

But he stayed put. The cheerful voice, the creamy porridge (his own was always lumpy) and—wonder of wonders!—the hiss of flapjacks poured onto the hot griddle held him spellbound in his chair. "I declare!" he said more than once, shaking his head, as Samantha described the rescue, two years before, of the tiny inhabitants of Dopple.

The late Professor Kurtz's late nephew had, she said, carried on as Professor Lilliput upon his uncle's death. At the time of his arrest he had suffered a nervous collapse brought on by a towering fit of astonishment and rage and been put away in an institution that specialized in helping the collapsed. Soon afterward, the trustees assigned by the court to manage his estate (since he was judged both too ill and too wicked to do so himself) had signed a contract with Mammoth Business Machines (better known as MBM) to do the research necessary to perfect the Reducer as a reliable tool for scientific use. The provisions of the contract were confidential, but Mr. Augustus Dopple, who was a trustee, had once intimated that fees and royalties would eventually lead to a yearly income in the millions. Poor Kurtzes! Fortune had smiled, but fortunately late.

Pete took in less than half of this. When Samantha went on to say something about "the others being due about now," Pete only chuckled, shook his head, and waggled his fork. "Little Samantha, by jinks!"

Samantha eyed him doubtfully and wondered whether the shock had been too much.

Her worry was wasted. The minute Pete caught sight of her car, a Land Rover, parked on the front-porch side of the house, he was all for driving out to meet the visitors who had been waiting down at the Sampson place for eight o'clock and Samantha's "All Clear."

"Lest they miss that turn up top the gully," he said hastily, resisting the temptation to give one of the heavy tires a test kick. They couldn't be that fat and solid rubber. One of the newfangled innertube sort, he allowed. "Road's pretty bad overgrowed there."

Samantha agreed and left the dishes in the sink. As they bucketed along the churned-up road, Pete was full of admiration. The old mule wagon would have been shaken to bits at half the speed. His barrage of questions about horsepower, self-starters, and gear ratios wavered only once, when a strong young scrub oak, which had been buried under the two feet of topsoil that had been replaced when the farm was restored to its former area, broke up through the potato patch, pattering dirt in all directions like a feeble catapult.

At the head of the gully, where the road had long since been washed out by Old Way Creek, Pete and Samantha met a battered red jeep and an astonishing number—astonishing to Pete, at least—of people on foot. A Mrs. Bright, and Augustus Dopple, a thin old gentleman of eighty or so, were passengers in the jeep. Mindy Hallam and her parents, Samantha's brother Ed, and two youngish gentlemen in business suits came just behind. The two strangers were introduced as Dr. O. P. Pennyman, Director of Research and Development at Mammoth Business Machines, and his colleague, Dr. Marion. Bringing up the rear were the Brittlesdale police constable, Edward Beagle, and stout red-faced Sheriff Henry Binns.

Samantha leaned on the steering wheel and grinned hugely at everyone's astonishment. "Impossible," they had said. And, "No one could survive cut off so long. But tall, gangly, berry-brown, blue-eyed Pete MacCubbin was just as agog at them.

Sheriff Binns pushed forward. "Pete? Pete MacCubbin?" he wheezed, mopping his forehead with a blue bandanna. "By all that's holy, it *is* you! Old Petey. Don't you know me, Pete? Hank Binns. Skinny Binns. In old lady Ample's class, remember?" He pumped Pete's hand vigorously. "I'm mighty glad these folks dragged me up here after all. Wouldn't explain—just said somebody who knew the MacCubbins ought to come along. Folks always said you'd all gone off to Detroit. How long you been back?"

Everyone talked at once. Pete, seizing a chance to

sidle off unnoticed, poked around the jeep and managed a quick look under the hood before someone plucked at his elbow to draw him after the others.

They had questions about everything: the animals' shyness, the roofless barn, the fields sprouting half-smothered trees. The general dilapidation suddenly struck Pete. Overnight his tidy farm had taken on a sadly ramshackle look. The sheds sagged and the old hen coop listed drunkenly, where yesterday they had been shabby but trim. "What—" he began in indignant protest.

"I can guess what you're thinking, Mr. MacCubbin," said Dr. Marion quietly in his ear. "Unavoidable, I'm afraid. The Reducer can only magnify what it minified. Any repairs you made with materials from the woods beyond your own boundaries wouldn't hold. Shingles, logs, planks—they were really only sticks and shavings. Hard on you, sir, I know, but it's a necessary safety precaution. Otherwise you might have got your farm back complete with oversize insects and giant birds. Mustn't tamper with nature, you know."

He smiled. "No need to worry. You can afford to build as many barns as you want now."

That took Banker Dopple to explain. By a fluke the late Professor had not foreseen, Pete, it seemed was the sole beneficiary of Kurtz's fortune.

Nephew Kurtz, in sound mind at the very last, had gnashed his teeth at the thought of his new fortune going to the State of Pennsylvania. He had no heir, and though for spite he would have liked to leave everything to a Society for the Abolition of Pets, he wished to give his enemies no chance to contest his will

(132)

in court with a charge that he had still been of unsound mind. At last, with a self-satisfied chuckle, he drew up and had witnessed a will leaving everything in perpetual trust "for those Poor Souls among the victims of my Uncle who are now or are later found to be in Reduced Circumstances." The pun gave him another chuckle—not because he knew of the Reducer's midnight trek to the MacCubbin farm, but because it was a nice malicious touch. None of those prosperous New Dopple folk could touch a penny of his millions-to-be!

It was all too much for a body to take in. While his guests poked and explored, Pete headed for the kitchen. He needed a cup of strong black coffee!

Fourteen

THEY WERE STILL IN THE KITCHEN AN HOUR LATER: SA-
mantha sampling the tiny dabs of rose hip and May-
apple marmalade, pepperroot relish, violet jelly, and
pickled wild mint left at the bottom of the preserving
jars. The jars of applesauce and pickled vegetables,
from the lost farm's own trees and seed, were full; but
all of the preserves made from wild things gathered in
the woods across the Waste had, like the back steps replaced with woods lumber, been passed over during
the Magnification.

"Good thing it wasn't winter," Pete chuckled.
"I'd've froze. My winter suit's made of moleskin."

Samantha's eyes twinkled. "Lucky," she said. "But
too bad there's so little left of *this*." She licked the
spoon. "Delicious. What is it? Mushrooms?"

Pete sniffed at the jar. "That's it. Pickled inkies."

"And all the recipes are in your Granny's book?"

They were bent over the kitchen table, leafing through the book, when old Mrs. Bright and young Mindy came to fetch them. Mrs. Bright seeing the two graying heads so close together, and the two pairs of sparkling blue eyes, smiled to herself.

Mindy sailed right in. "Everybody's ready to go, and we're supposed to collect you. Mr. MacCubbin's invited to stay at our house until his roof's fixed."

"Unless," Mrs. Bright amended, "it would be too-much-all-at-once, Mr. MacCubbin."

"Nope." Pete pushed his chair back, stuck out his long legs, and eyed his patchwork trousers and gaping homemade boots. "I reckon Samantha and me can stop in at Mosstown on the way and get me a pair of overalls and some store-bought clodhoppers. Don't want folks to think somebody's scarecrow's broke loose."

With everyone cheerfully piled into the two vehicles for the trip down the ridge, Mindy was heard to say what most of them were thinking.

"Isn't it great"—she sighed contentedly—"that it's a happy ending?"

"Not a loose end in sight," her father teased.

Old Mrs. Bright smiled to herself. There was *one* knot still to be tied . . . She would be willing to bet on it.

And so there was. The first inkling anyone had of it came in the mail several months later on a large card tastefully lettered in greens and browns:

Village Foods, Brittlesdale
and
The Beacon Dairy, Johnstown

Are proud to announce that from September 1st
They will be carrying an exciting new line
of pickles, preserves, and syrups

from
GRANNY MACCUBBIN'S CUPBOARD
Authentic Folk Recipes   Wild Woods Flavors

Grown, gathered, and prepared
At Samantha and Peter MacCubbin's
Found Again Farm,
Mosstown, R. D. 2.